An Unforeseen Danger

A. K. Gentry

Brushy Mountain Publications

ISBN Print: 979-8-9888618-4-3

ISBN Digital: 979-8-9888618-5-0

Library of Congress Number: 2024925985

Book Cover by Marissa Mueller at MAM Crafted   Instagram @mamcrafted1

Editing by Margaret Griffin at margaretgriffinbooks@gmail.com

CONTENTS

NOTE TO THE READER

Like the other books I have written, this one is a clean romance with no graphic violence. However, the subject of stalking, sexual predators, and crimes against women are part of the plot. This book also deals with the fortitude of one woman to fight back against such criminals.

Thank you for reading.

A. K. Gentry

CHAPTER 1

<hr>

G rant Sparks inhaled the aroma of his fresh cup of coffee before taking that first sip. An unusually cool summer breeze rose up from the street and across the balcony where he was sitting. The breeze brought the aroma of bacon from the cafe on the floor below him, reminding him that he had not yet eaten breakfast.

Taking a careful sip of the hot coffee, Grant smiled, enjoying the fresh start to a new day. He sighed with contentment as he looked down on Main Street in Whitlow. He had lived here for almost a year, and he liked it. Whitlow was a quaint, small southern town with a blend of the historical and the modern.

Across the street was the historical old bank building that had been renovated to house a bakery, an event center, and the offices of Garner Logistics where he now worked. The lights in the bakery and on the third floor made Grant think about his journey to this moment.

His former job had been at an electronics firm in the neighboring town of Troy. The business closed due to the owner's mismanagement, and Grant had worried about paying his bills until his friend and neighbor, Tracy, called him about this job. Tracy managed Candy's Café which was on the floor below him.

Paul Garner owned Garner Logistics and originally lived in Grant's apartment. He decided that his business had grown enough that he needed an assistant who was good with computers. After Tracy had given Paul's information to Grant, he called Paul. They met, and Grant was hired. He now had the best job he could have wanted.

At first Grant ran logistical schedules between merchants, manufacturers and freight haulers. It was a successful company, but he had streamlined it in such a way that both vendors and freight haulers lowered costs and increased profits. Between Paul's marketing and the word of mouth that spread through the industries, the company had become even more successful, doubling in size. Grant was now the general manager of Garner Logistics and had an assistant helping him.

Originally, Grant commuted to Whitlow from Troy for his job during his first two years of employment. When Paul and his wife, Candy, moved into the new house they built on a local farm, Paul offered Grant the chance to rent his apartment. Grant didn't think twice about moving to Whitlow. Living this close to the office was convenient. He usually chuckled when he told anyone about his commute; he just walked across the street. All his friends back in Troy were jealous of that.

Grant liked his office on the third floor of the old bank building. He and his assistant, Bailey, had the whole floor to themselves. Occasionally the aroma of pastries drifted up the stairs from Candy's bakery to his office. It always made his stomach growl, and he had to be disciplined to keep from going downstairs for a snack.

The alarm on his watch broke Grant's train of thought. It was only eight o'clock. His office hours were eight to five with an hour for lunch, but he was responsible for keeping the on-call phone manned until eight pm in case a client called. He and Bailey had flexible hours to handle this. Tonight was his turn for the on-call, so he didn't rush across the street. Bailey had texted him that she was there, which meant he could enjoy another cup of coffee.

Grant leaned back in his chair as he sipped his second cup of coffee. It was quiet. The only vehicles on Main Street were people going to the cafe or the bakery. It was much busier during the school year. The elementary school was just down the street, and during the school year, traffic was slow as cars and buses waited their turn to get into the parking lot.

Movement on the balcony on the bank building caught his attention. It looked like some birds were trying to build a nest. He would let Paul know. Paul owned that building plus the one beside it through his property management company, Blue Ridge Properties. It seemed like Paul and his brother, Chip, were single handedly renovating the town of Whitlow. Grant smiled. Paul loved balconies, so he guessed more would be appearing on Main Street.

Grant quickly drank the rest of his now cooled coffee. This day may be flexible, but there were still things he needed to get done since it was Monday. Grant gathered his computer bag, locked his apartment and went downstairs to the cafe. He bought a sausage biscuit and an iced tea then walked across the street. Time to get to work.

CHAPTER 2

Kelli Mills nervously checked her appearance in the mirror as she finished getting ready. It was her first day in her new job with Cotton Catering and Events, and she wanted to make a good impression. She pulled her strawberry blond hair back into an efficient ponytail, added a dab of blusher on her cheeks, and put the mascara on her lashes. Finally, her makeup was finished, and Kelli put everything back in its place in the bathroom.

Going to her bedroom closet, Kelli chose black dress pants with a light blue silk blouse and black flats. She knew there would be days when blue jeans and athletic shoes would be the dress of the day, but not today.

Since graduating from college with a degree in hospitality management, Kelli had worked at several different hotels and convention centers. Her last job had been in the middle management of a large convention center where she scheduled events and vendors. She liked the job, but she didn't enjoy living in the large city where it was located. Everything there was loud and fast paced, and it seemed to her that life's stressors were always running on high. She preferred a quieter, slower paced town.

Frustrated with that situation, Kelli started searching the internet for a similar job in a suburban or a small-town setting. Unable to believe her eyes, she saw the ad for an event coordinator in Whitlow, North Carolina. She responded immediately and within a week had an appointment for an interview. The trip to Whitlow had taken her five hours to drive, but it was worth it when she saw the town.

Kelli fell in love with Whitlow on her first drive down Main Street. Crepe myrtle trees of all colors lined the street. In between the trees and on every corner were concrete raised beds of flowers. She could tell the buildings were old and historical. Several had been renovated and a few more were in the process of being restored. The only thing missing from the perfect job in the perfect town was a place to live. Kelli got the job, moved to Whitlow and signed a temporary lease with a motel near the interstate that had suites for extended stays, but she hoped she could eventually find a rental inside the city limits.

The historic building in which Kelli was to work had a private parking area behind it. She arrived on time and parked her small SUV in a designated spot. Looking up, Kelli could see the unique outer facade of the old building. The windows were new as well as the large industrial back door, which looked very secure. Excited, Kelli gathered her purse and computer bag. She took a deep breath and got out of her car. The first day on a job was always nerve wracking no matter how competent she was for the position, but she was determined to quash the nerves and enjoy the experience. As arranged, she entered the back door and walked down a hallway to the bakery.

Candy Garner had been at the bakery since six am baking muffins and cinnamon rolls, filling display cases, and making coffee. She made sure everything was in place for opening the store at seven. The first two hours were usually the busiest as people stopped in for coffee and a muffin or cinnamon bun on the way to school or work. She smiled when she saw Kelli coming into the front dining area.

Candy wiped her hands and came around the display cases.

"Kelli!" she exclaimed, "welcome to your first day on the new job. How do you like Whitlow so far?"

"I love Whitlow," Kelli said. "It's like the idyllic town from a romance novel or something. I had no idea such places existed."

Candy smiled, "We love it. I was raised here, but Paul, my husband, wasn't. He and his brother, Chip, are from Philadelphia. Moving to a small southern town was a culture shock for them, but they've adjusted. Have you had breakfast?"

"Yes, thank you," Kelli replied.

"One perk of this job will be all the coffee you want," Candy said pointing to the urns along the wall. "We may even be able to accommodate you with a muffin," she added, winking. "I guess you're ready to get started, so come on back to my office."

Kelli followed Candy through the bakery to the office in back. She sat across from Candy at the desk and filled out the initial employment paperwork.

*****

Paul Garner entered the old bank building from the back and climbed the stairs to the third floor. He owned Garner Logistics and Blue Ridge Properties. He usually worked from home, but he was frequently at the building to discuss business with Grant and to see Candy, his wife, who owned the bakery.

Opening the door from the stairwell to the third floor, Paul walked into a small lobby, which now served as the office for Bailey, Grant's assistant.

"Morning, Bailey. Is Grant in?" Paul asked.

"Yes. He just got here; he has the on-call tonight," Bailey answered.

Paul walked down the short hall to the large office in the rear and knocked on the door.

"Grant, it's Paul."

"Come in," Grant answered.

Paul walked in. Grant had several pieces of paper scattered on his desk. His eyes were glued to the computer and one finger kept his place on a list.

"How's it going?" Paul asked.

"Good," Grant answered, turning to face Paul. "I'm working on the connections between vendors in the southwest. One has expanded and needs freight hauled into Colorado and Montana." He smiled, "More business for us."

"Are things still working out well with Bailey?" Paul asked.

"Yes," Grant said. "She's great. I gave her the responsibility of moving the products for vendors in the northeastern states. She handles it like a charm. I'm going to increase her workload soon. If she can handle the incremental increases as well as I think she can, we can delay hiring another person. I'm afraid there wouldn't be enough work, yet, for two assistants even though it would be nice to have another person to share the on-call evenings."

"Sounds good," Paul replied. "Keep me informed as to how it's going. I'm flying out to Spokane, Washington later this week to talk with a manufacturer there. I need to find a freight company nearby willing to contract with us, so I may be there a few days."

"OK. Don't worry about the office. We'll be fine," Grant said.

"I have no worries," Paul said smiling. "I came to talk to you about something else, though."

"Yeah?" Grant asked. "What's on your mind."

"I need to use the empty office in the hallway," Paul said.

"Okay. It's your building. Who's moving in?" Grant asked.

"Kelli Mills," Paul said. "Candy's having trouble juggling everything with the way the catering and events businesses are growing. She hired Kelli to be an events coordinator. Tracy will still manage the café, and Kelli will coordinate the catering and events. They will have to work together because the café will still do the cooking for the catered meals for now. Candy is even concerned she may need to find another kitchen if the catering continues to grow."

"I'm going to let Kelli use the hallway office for a while since there's no other available space," Paul said. "Once she gets adjusted, she probably won't be here much. The catering phone number is a cell phone, so she can answer that anywhere."

Paul watched a look of unease growing on Grant's face. He hoped Grant would be willing to give this arrangement a chance.

"What do we do if we eventually hire a third person for Garner Logistics?" Grant asked, his brow furrowed with concern.

"We'll address that issue when it arises," Paul answered.

"You don't expect Bailey to play hostess if someone comes in to see this girl about a party or a reception, do you?" Grant asked. "A constant stream of people coming and going could break her concentration. Shouldn't she have the office and this girl have the area in front?"

Paul replied, "We thought it would be better if Kelli had an office where she could shut the door if she's talking with a customer. Grant, let's just see how it works out. If you feel it's jeopardizing Garner Logistics, let me know. I would rather change the office situation than have any mistakes or issues with scheduling our clients. It won't be long before offices are available in one of the adjoining buildings we're renovating. We can always move the logistics company to the new building and let Candy's businesses all be housed here."

Paul knew there were potential problems that a lot of foot traffic and noise could create for Grant and Bailey, and he tried to convey his support to Grant. He was relieved when he saw some of the worry lessen in Grant's face.

"All right," Grant said. "We'll see how it goes."

Chapter 3

Candy took the signed employment forms from Kelli. "Now that the official paperwork is finished, we can get to the fun part," she said with a wide smile as she stood. "Let me show you around."

"You've seen the bakery," Candy said as she came around the desk. "The kitchen is larger than the cafe's, but the sitting area is much smaller. Let me show you the second floor."

Candy led Kelli out of a side door into the public hallway that housed the elevator. They rode up to the second floor where the door opened to the large empty area.

Kelli looked around at the shiny wooden floors, open space, and neutral walls. The original crown molding had been kept, keeping a vintage look to the ceiling. Antique looking chandeliers hung from the ceiling between recessed lights. A staging area had been blocked off just to the left of the elevator, and restrooms were behind a screen at the back of the room. Kelli walked over to the double doors that allowed access to the balcony.

"What's the occupancy allowed in here?" she asked.

"We're allowed one hundred people at any one time,"

Candy said. "Paul is renovating the building next door. He's in the process of discussing with the contractor and an engineer the possibility of removing the wall between the buildings so we can expand this venue. Then we can have larger events."

"I hope it's feasible," Kelli said, smiling. "This would be a great place for a high school prom or a large wedding reception."

"I know," Candy replied as she opened the elevator door. "Now, let's go to the third floor. That's where your office will be. Currently, those offices are for Garner Logistics, but there's one that is empty, and we thought you could use it for now. Grant and Bailey concentrate heavily on what they're doing, and since they're the only ones on that floor, they aren't used to any noise. If our business causes problems for them, we'll have to rethink who works where, but Paul and I decided to try it for a while, at least until the other buildings are finished. Come on, we'll go up the elevator and come back down the stairs, so you'll know your way around."

The elevator opened onto the third floor allowing Candy and Kelli to walk into the lobby. Kelli saw a young woman with short dark hair and dark eyes sitting at the desk, which had papers scattered across the top.

"Bailey," Candy said, "this is Kelli Mills. She's going to use the hall office for now. Kelli, this is Bailey Jenkins. She works with Paul and Grant for Garner Logistics."

"It's nice to meet you, Bailey," Kelli said smiling.

"It's nice to meet you too, Kelli," Bailey answered. "I hope you'll like working here."

"I'm sure I will," Kelli replied.

Candy smiled at Bailey then turned to Kelli, "Your office is this way," and Candy led Kelli down the hall. Candy opened the door to an office with a desk and an office chair in the middle of the floor.

"This is all that's in here for the moment," Candy said. "We can add whatever you need. I'm guessing that a filing cabinet will be in order, because I'm going to turn all the paperwork for the catering and events businesses over to you. The phone number for the business goes to a cell phone. Remind me to get that to you today. It usually stays with Ellen, the employee downstairs in the bakery."

Candy went back into the hallway and proceeded to the office at the back of the building. The nameplate on the closed door read, 'Grant Sparks, General Manager.' Candy knocked on the door.

"Come in," Grant answered.

Candy opened the door to see Paul sitting in the chair opposite Grant's desk.

"Oh," she said, "am I interrupting?"

"No. Come in," Paul answered.

Candy ushered Kelli into the room and said, "Kelli, this is Paul, my husband."

Kelli watched a tall, handsome man with black hair and blue eyes stand and smile at her.

"Kelli, it's great to meet you," Paul said has he shook Kelli's hand. "I'm glad you're here to take some of the load off Candy. It was all getting to be too much work for her to handle."

"It's nice to meet you," Kelli said. "I'm excited to be here. I already love Whitlow."

Candy motioned to the man behind the desk. Kelli noted his light brown hair and green eyes.

"Kelli this is Grant Sparks, the general manager for the

logistics company," Candy said.

Grant stood and shook Kelli's hand, "Nice to meet you, Kelli."

"It's nice to meet you, too," Kelli answered, noting that he was almost as tall as Paul.

"Well," Candy said as she turned to the door, "we're going across the street so I can introduce Kelli to Tracy. You two carry on with whatever you were doing." She smiled and waved as she closed the door behind them.

Standing in the middle of the hallway, Candy pointed to the door closest to Grant's office.

"That one is the restroom," she said, "and this one beside it is the stairwell." Candy took Kelli to the second floor to show her where the door accessed the room, then continued down the stairs.

"Before we go across the street, I want to show you the basement," Candy said and continued walking to the lowest level where she opened the large, heavy door.

Candy led Kelli into the basement area. Storage cabinets divided the room into large open spaces. Tables, chairs, and lattice panels were stacked along one wall haphazardly. Vases and candlesticks were scattered over two tables.

"The best advice I can give you is to take a day, wear old clothes, and explore," Candy said. "I'll give you an inventory. Don't be afraid to book a party for something out of the realm of what we have. Everything down here was ordered for something different. It has collected into quite a jumble."

Candy took Kelli back to the first floor using the elevator. Together, they left the building and walked across the street to the café. When they entered the café, Candy led

Kelli along the serving counter to the back of the dining room. A glass window on the office wall showed Tracy working at her desk.

When Candy walked into the room, Tracy stood and said, "Let me guess; this is Kelli."

"Yes," Candy said, smiling. "Kelli, this is Tracy. She manages the café and the meals-to-go business. The food for the catered events will come from here, so the two of you will need to work closely together. I have standard menus to give you, but it's always good to touch base with Tracy about pricing before you meet with a potential customer."

"Tracy, it's nice to meet you," Kelli said, smiling. "Be reassured, I'm used to checking with a chef and the kitchen about availability before booking any new business. It makes for a much easier life for us all."

Candy closed the office door then sat and talked with both women outlining the changes and expansion she was planning for Cotton Catering and Events.

*****

Grant watched Paul walk down the hall and leave the office. He was not happy. The last thing he wanted was an event planner disrupting his concentration with telephone calls. He walked down the hall to Bailey's desk.

"What did you think of Candy's new employee?" he asked her.

"She seemed nice," Bailey answered.

"I don't like that Paul gave her that office instead of you," he said. "I had planned to move you there when we eventually hired the third person. I'm worried that traffic out here will make you lose concentration. If it becomes a problem, let me know. I'll talk to Paul about it."

"Okay," Bailey answered, "but I don't think she'll be here that much. It seems to me she will be doing most of her business with clients on the second floor, or rummaging around the basement, or across the street with Tracy. Besides, she seemed nice. I liked her."

"I'm glad you liked her, but I'm not happy about the situation, and I made that known to Paul. We're used to quiet so we can concentrate." Grant gave a disgusted sigh and walked back to his office.

*****

Later that afternoon, the elevator opened, and Kelli pushed a hand truck piled high with boxes into the third floor lobby.

"Hey, Bailey. I guess I'm moving in," she said smiling.

"Hey," Bailey responded. "Looks like you are. That's a lot of boxes."

"There are still a few more," Kelli said as she pushed the hand truck to her office and unloaded the boxes onto the floor. She jumped, startled, when she heard the door to Grant's office slam shut. Kelli rolled her eyes. If he's that annoyed with one hand truck full of files, how's he going to react with more noise.

"See you in a bit with the rest of my load," Kelli said to Bailey as she pushed the empty handtruck through the lobby and onto the elevator.

Bailey nodded, still looking at her screen.

Ten minutes later, Kelli returned with another load of boxes, not as tall as the first.

"This is the last," she said to Bailey. "I hope I don't

bother you again today."

"No worries," Bailey said with a grin. "I seem to be able to tune you out and keep working. Hope you aren't offended."

"Offended? No way," Kelli said. "I'm glad you can do that." Kelli pointed to Grant's door and said, "Mr. Personality doesn't seem to have the same talent. Is he always this irritable?"

"No," Bailey answered, shaking her head. "Grant's great. He's a nice guy and super to work for. I think he's just worried about losing concentration if your business grows and there's a lot of noise out here."

Grant heard their conversation. It was hard not to since neither one of the girls bothered to lower their voices. So, Miss Cheerful thought he was irritable. The woman hadn't seen irritable. Wait until she made him mad or caused him or Bailey to make a mistake. Then she would see more than irritable.

Kelli handed Bailey a business card, "Candy had these made for me. If you need coffee, call me. I'll bring you one from the bakery on my way up the elevator."

"Really?" Bailey asked with a wide smile. "Super, I love the white chocolate creamer Candy keeps down there. Thanks."

"Do you think Grant would want a coffee in the mornings?" Kelli asked.

Bailey looked down the hall at the closed door.

"Hand me another card," Bailey said with her palm outstretched. "I'll ask him when he comes out. He usually brings his own from home, which is the apartment over the café. Don't be offended if he never asks."

"I won't," Kelli said. "No worries."

Kelli took the stack of boxes to her office and unloaded them on the floor next to the others. She surveyed the office and decided to move the desk to a corner to leave more room for chairs for clients.

Grant heard her moving furniture.

He snarled softly, "This is just great. Now she's moving furniture. What else will she be doing?" Finally, the noise stopped.

Kelli opened one of the boxes and pulled the calendar out. She studied how Candy had organized it and what the upcoming events were. Looking around the room she knew she needed a filing cabinet and a wall calendar. She was a visual person and liked using a calendar that showed a whole year at a glance. She grabbed the hand truck and took it back to the basement.

Candy looked up from a tray of partially decorated cookies when Kelli came back into the bakery.

"How's it going?" she asked, laying her piping bag to the side.

"Good," Kellie answered. "Would it be okay if I went to the office supply store and got a filing cabinet and some wall calendars?"

"Sure, let me give you something." Candy wiped her hands, walked back to the office and took a credit card from the top drawer. "This is a credit card for catering and events. Use it to get what you need. Just bring me the receipts."

"Where did you take potential customers to discuss what they wanted?" Kelli asked.

"I was all over the place with that," Candy said. "You need a nice comfortable, consistent place for appointments. Get a small table and some nice chairs for your office. We can start with that. If things get busier, we can rethink it."

"Okay. I promise I won't go all high end on you," Kelli said smiling.

Candy smiled and said, "Somehow, I didn't think you would. You seem very sensible and down to earth. That's one reason you got the job. Some of the people I interviewed were very pretentious, and I thought they looked down their nose at a small-town business."

"Uh, I know the type," Kelli said. "They really got on my nerves when I had to work with them. Well, I'm going to take care of that errand. I'll see you tomorrow." Kelli took her keys from her purse and started toward the back door.

"Okay," Candy replied. "Have a nice evening, and Kelli, I'm glad you're here."

Kelli smiled, "I'm glad I'm here, too. I can't wait to get things going." She waved and walked out the back door.

CHAPTER 4

G rant sighed with frustration. The morning quiet had been shattered with Kelli's voice as she gave Bailey a cup of coffee. The woman didn't know the word whisper; he was sure of it. Finally things had quieted down, and he could get back to work.

The phone rang, and Grant answered it. One of their largest vendors in Chicago needed transportation for a significant order to New Orleans. Grant was quietly discussing the issue with the company when the elevator door opened and he heard Kelli talking with two men. They talked so loudly that he had a hard time hearing his caller.

Grant was grateful that the conversation in the hallway was short, and he easily completed his call. Settling back into his chair, the elevator doors opened again. This time Grant heard Bailey talking to the men. Curious, he got up and opened his door. He saw a man carrying chairs and another one rolling a large box on a hand truck. Everything went into Kelli's office.

Things quieted, the men left the floor, and Grant went back to his desk. Ten minutes later, the elevators opened a third time, and the two men were back. Grant opened his door again to see one carrying a large Ficus tree, and the other carried three wall hangings. As he was standing there, Kelli exited the elevator and thanked the delivery men as they were leaving. She started walking to her office.

Kelli saw Grant at his door. When her eyes met his, she paused and said, "Good morning, Grant."

"Are you through with the movers?" Grant asked brusquely.

"If you mean the delivery men, then yes, they're finished," Kelli replied.

"Good," Grant said, "I trust we will return to quiet?"

"I suppose so," Kelli answered. "I'm sorry if I disturbed you. It was only three trips up the elevator."

"Three trips too many," Grant mumbled in annoyance and closed his door.

Her good mood and happiness were briefly marred by Grant's sour comments, but Kelli turned to her office and became excited again. She took a utility knife and cut the box off her filing cabinet. Then she moved it into place behind her desk.

Grant heard every move Kelli made in the next office. He knew exactly what she was doing. She was so loud it couldn't be secret. Grant got up and walked out to see Bailey.

"Has all this bothered you?" he asked.

"Not really," Bailey answered. "After the first trip up, I tuned them out. Why? Is it bothering you?"

"It's distracting and annoying," he said.

"It's only one time," Bailey said. "She had to move in. I made some noise, too, the first day I came to work."

"But that was different," Grant replied. "You were working for me." He turned, walked back down the hall, went into his office and closed the door.

Kelli came out of her office carrying cardboard.

She passed Bailey and said, "I'm going to the recycling bin. Do you have anything to go?"

"No, thank you," Bailey replied.

"Did I get you into trouble?" Kelli asked. "I heard Grant come out here to talk to you."

"No," Bailey replied. "It's fine."

Kelli pushed the button for the elevator.

"He sure has a short attention span if I can bother him that easily." The door opened and Kelli disappeared into the small space.

Bailey giggled. Grant with a short attention span? If she only knew. The man could focus for hours.

Grant heard the comment Kelli had made. Short attention span? She accused him of having a short attention span? Unbelievable! He wished there was some way of getting her out of this office.

Kelli took the cardboard to the recycle bin, then went to her SUV to get the rest of her purchases from the office supply store. This time when she exited the elevator she didn't speak. She just waved to Bailey.

Inside the office, Kelli rolled up her sleeves and began to work. She filed everything that had been in the boxes Candy gave her. She decided her desk was in the wrong place, so she moved it from the corner to the center of the back wall; then she used the small table to make an extension to the desk. Kelli placed the chairs in front of the desk and put the Ficus tree in a corner of the room.

Grant was so annoyed that he couldn't concentrate.

She was moving the desk again. She opened and closed filing cabinet drawers so many times he thought he was going to go in there and throttle her. Then she was dragging chairs across the carpet. He would bet Paul had no idea how thin the inside walls were in this office.

When Kelli started nailing tacks into the wall, Grant looked up to see the map on his wall shaking. He lost his temper and stormed out of his office and into hers.

"What are you doing?" he shouted as he stepped through the open door.

Kelli jumped in surprise. She turned to face him.

"Hanging up my calendars. I have permission to do so," she informed him.

"I don't care if you have permission or not!" Grant exclaimed. "Stop! You're making way too much noise."

Kelli started to get annoyed.

"Grant, I'm sorry," Kelli said as she finished nailing a tack. "It's only one day to move in and get the office set up. I'll be done before long."

"I said stop making noise," Grant said angrily through a clenched jaw.

"I will when I'm finished." Kelli said firmly, "and I'm almost done. It won't be long, and it will all be over. If I stop now, then I will just have to start again later."

"I don't care if you never finish. Stop hammering!" he demanded.

"Not until I'm finished. I only have two tacks left," she replied firmly.

The elevator doors sounded. Candy came down the hall and saw Grant glaring at Kelli and Kelli glaring back.

"Do we have a problem?" Candy asked.

Kelli turned to Candy and said, "No. We were just discussing the calendars I'm going to hang on the wall."

"Oh, I want to see those," Candy said as she walked into the office. "I wish I had done that when I first started the business."

Kelli gave Grant a smirk of a smile then followed Candy into the room.

Grant muttered a low expletive and returned to his office. He couldn't compete with the boss's wife. Somehow, that seemed unfair.

When the hammering started again, Grant closed his computer, picked up his papers and walked down the hall.

He looked at Bailey and said, "I'm going home to work if you need me."

"OK," Bailey answered. She never looked up from her computer.

Candy looked at the wall. Three large calendars covered the space and held twelve months. The material was dry erase, and Kelli could label and reuse each month several times.

"This is huge!" Candy exclaimed, "and you can write a lot in the blocks."

Kelli nodded. "I have everything in detail on the computer and my phone. But this gives me a visual of everything in one glance. I love these things."

Paul stepped off the elevator and into the lobby. Bailey did not look up. He walked down the hall to Grant's office and knocked on the door. When there was no answer, he opened the door and found the office empty. Confused, Paul went back down the hall to Bailey.

"Did Grant leave?" he asked.

Bailey looked up.

"Yes," she answered. "He said he was going home to work. I think the noise got to him."

"Did it get to you?" Paul asked.

"I tuned it out. I'm pretty good at that," Bailey answered.

Huh, Paul thought. So, Grant did have a weakness and an Achilles Heel. He never thought he would find one.

"I think it was the hammering on the wall that got to him," Bailey said. "But it was just six tacks. It was over in less than two minutes. I honestly think Kelli got on his nerves as much as the noise."

"Really?" Paul asked. "What makes you think that?"

"I made the same noise the day I started to work here, but it didn't bother him at all. The difference is Kelli," Bailey said.

"I guess you're right," Paul replied. "I hope he adjusts."

Paul walked down the hall and into Kelli's office. There was disorder with the promise of becoming organized. Candy was there going over the schedules for the next several months.

Candy looked up, "Oh, hey, Honey. Why are you here?"

"I came up to see Grant, but he left," Paul answered.

"He did?" Candy asked, surprised. "He rarely does that."

"That may have been my fault," Kelli said with a sheepish look. "Between the trips made by the delivery men and my hammering tacks, he was pretty upset with me. I told him it was temporary and that I wouldn't be making so much noise again. Hopefully, he will be happier about everything tomorrow."

"Don't worry about it," Paul said. "It'll all work out." He turned and left the offices.

"I hope he can adjust," Candy said. "If not, you may have the whole floor to yourself."

"I promise to be quieter," Kelli said. "Today was just unusual."

"I believe you," Candy said. "Now, can you come downstairs? I have some things down there I want to go over with you."

Kelli followed Candy to her office on the first floor.

*****

Grant was working at his dining room table. It was almost five. He had the cell phone with the on-call phone number. He was going to be tied down for the next three hours, so he might as well get some work done. Staring out the sliding glass doors to the bakery building across the street, Grant had trouble concentrating. He was still annoyed, but this time he couldn't blame it on noise. He blamed Kelli herself. Everything had been smooth and efficient until Paul gave her that office. If her job had been like his, it would have been fine. Instead, she was going to be a disruption. He hoped the company didn't suffer because of her ability to break his and Bailey's concentration.

CHAPTER 5

The weekend had finally arrived. Grant finished dressing and frowned at the gray that was starting to show at his temples. Thanks Dad. His father had been prematurely gray by the age of forty. His complexion caught his attention in the mirror. Raising a hand to his face, Grant thought he looked pale. He never seemed to get outside any more, and it was summer. He should be bugging his cousin to take the boat out on the lake.

Grant covered his green eyes with sunglasses and walked out to his car. He started the engine and pulled out of the parking lot behind the cafe. He was driving the ten miles back to Troy. His best friend's parents were having a fiftieth wedding anniversary party at the Senior Center. The Rosser's had been like second parents to him, and he wouldn't miss their big moment for anything.

Candy drove the utility van with the food and drinks to the Senior Center in Troy.

"I'm going to show you the ropes and introduce you to the catering staff," she told Kelli. "After that, it's all yours."

"That's what you hired me for," Kelli said, smiling.

Candy backed the van to the loading area outside the kitchen. She made sure the doors to the center were unlocked, and they started unloading the food and supplies.

Candy looked up to see a young woman with a brunette ponytail standing on the loading dock.

"Trisha!" she exclaimed. "Right on time. Can you help with the unloading?"

"Sure," Trisha replied.

When she reached the van, Candy said, "Trisha, this is Kelli Mills. She's the new manager for the catering service."

"Nice to meet you, Kelli," Trisha said as she picked up a tray of food.

"It's nice to meet you too," Kelli said and took a stack of tablecloths inside.

Soon, the women had the buffet table set up and the kitchen prepped to make refilling the serving pans easier. Two more employees came in and were introduced to Kelli. All of them wore black pants, white shirts, and full length black aprons with Cotton Catering and Events and the cotton boll logo monogrammed in silver.

The time for dinner was getting near. The main course of meat and vegetables was placed over the hot water reservoirs. Salad was placed near the plates and bread was put at the opposite end of the table. A separate table held pieces of carrot cake, pecan pie, and large sugar cookies.

While the attendees were arriving, servers mingled with trays of appetizers. Two beverage tables were available for guests to serve themselves before dinner. The guests of honor were introduced, and they led the way through the buffet line.

Kelli watched from the kitchen as the serving staff kept the food pans, dessert table, and beverage glasses full. When she noticed that all the servers were occupied with tasks, she grabbed a pitcher of tea and one of water and began circulating. She started with the table where the guests of honor sat. Moving on to the next table, Kelli looked down to see a man listening intently to a story being told by the woman sitting beside him. It was Grant. She smiled as she refilled his glass and quietly moved on.

Grant felt someone by his side and realized it was a server refilling his tea glass. He looked up to say thank you, but she had moved on. He was surprised to see that it was Kelli. He hadn't realized that Candy's company was catering the meal. He watched her as she moved smoothly and gracefully from table to table as if she had been doing this for years. He thought that she probably had. She occasionally spoke to a guest, but mostly she quietly did her job without even being noticed.

When the meal was over and the speeches were being made, Kelli helped the staff remove the food and equipment from the buffet table. They closed the kitchen doors and began cleaning up. When the guests started to leave, they all went out to start cleaning off the tables.

Kelli was getting the dishes off the last table when she heard someone call her name. She looked up to see Grant walking toward her.

"Hello Grant," she said, smiling. "How do you know the guests of honor?"

"Their son, Derrick, has been my best friend since first grade," he replied. "They're like a second set of parents to me."

"That's wonderful," Kelli replied. "I know you're happy

for them."

"I am," he said. "Tell Candy the meal was fabulous, as usual."

"Thanks," Kelli said. "I'll tell her, but she's in the kitchen if you want to tell her yourself."

"No, I don't want to bother her," Grant said. "You can tell her for me." He turned to leave, "Have a nice evening, Kelli."

"You, too, Grant," she said. Kelli watched him leave thinking that he could be pleasant when he wanted to be.

Grant left thinking that Kelli might be more professional than he had first thought.

CHAPTER 6

Cotton Catering and Events.

On Monday morning, Grant was startled from his concentration by Kelli's voice. He had not even realized she was in the building. Blast it, did the woman not have a volume button to lower her voice?

Trying to concentrate, he was grateful when he heard her say, "Yes. I have your event on the calendar and the date set for your appointment to decide on the menu. See you then, goodbye."

Grant thought whole third floor echoed with silence when Kelli stopped talking. Thank goodness his door was closed. He was working on the last set of entries when Kelli's phone rang again.

"Cotton Catering and Events."

Grant sighed with annoyance.

After a pause Kelli said, "I'm sorry, but we already have an event booked that evening. I will be glad to give you another date." There was silence then, "I understand. I hope your wedding and reception are beautiful."

Silence again. Grant looked back at his screen. He was almost finished when Kelli's phone rang a third time.

"Cotton Catering and Events."

Grant was furious. This is ridiculous. How can anyone get any work done with that overly cheerful woman talking so loud in the next office. He heard her walking around in her office and then a scratching sound on the wall. Those calendars. They were hanging on the wall between their offices, and he could hear the scratching noise as she wrote on them.

When he heard Kelli say goodbye, Grant got up and stormed out of his office to Kelli's. Her door was open.

"Is it always going to be like this?" he asked.

"Good morning, Grant," she said with a smile. "Is what always going to be like what?"

"The phone, your talking, the noise," he said, raising his hands in frustration.

"No, probably not," Kelli answered. "It's Monday. The phone always rings a lot on Mondays. People get engaged over the weekend then call to book a reception. People get together and plan parties; they call on Monday. Sunday school classes plan Christmas parties; they call on Monday. Businesses usually call later in the week after a staff or board meeting to book a dinner. Why, is there a problem?"

"Yes," Grant growled. "Noise. Your phone. Your voice. The scratching on the wall. It's all distracting."

"What's scratching on your wall?" Kelli asked.

"I assume it happens when you write on that calendar of yours. Who uses wall calendars anymore? Use your computer," he said in a gruff, condescending tone.

"I do use my computer," Kelli said, bristling. "It has all the information on every booking, and it's sync'd to my phone. I use the calendar as a quick answer to people's booking date request. And what's wrong with my voice?"

"It's loud!" Grant exclaimed. In a calmer voice, he said, "Your phone is loud. Your scratching is loud. We can't concentrate, and we work in a business that requires a lot of it."

By now Kelli was angry. She had done nothing to Grant, and here he was standing at her door verbally abusing her and her work.

"Well, Mr. Attention Deficit Disorder, maybe you need meds to help you focus," Kelli replied as she narrowed her eyes at Grant. "Your ability to concentrate is not my problem. I have been hired to do a job, and I will do it well. That job requires a phone, a voice, and a cheerful attitude for customer relations. Get. Over. It."

"Get over it?" he asked. Grant was angry. He walked toward Kelli's desk, and his voice had gone up several decibels. "You need to quiet down."

"Stop. Both of you stop."

Grant and Kelli turned to see Bailey in the doorway.

"Your arguing is not helping anything," Bailey continued. "Grant, keep your door closed and use ear plugs. Kelli, close your door and put your ringer down a notch. We can work this out. I certainly don't think we want the Garners to work this out. They pay us to do that." Bailey turned and walked back to her desk.

Kelli got up, walked toward her door and forced Grant back into the hallway.

"What are you doing?" Grant asked.

"Closing my door." Kelli firmly closed the door in his face. She was angry, but she did as Bailey asked.

Grant felt a wave of air hit his face as the door closed. He was furious. She had closed the door in his face! No one had ever closed a door in his face before, and he was not going to let her be the first.

He opened the door and shouted, "Don't ever close a door in my face again."

Still standing by the door, Kelli looked at him and firmly said, "I do not answer to you, Grant Sparks, and I just did what an employee in your company asked me to do, because I am a nice person. I do not work for Garner Logistics. I work for Cotton Catering and Events, so you cannot order me around. Get used to it."

Candy and Paul were on the second floor with an engineer who was looking to see if they could open the wall between the two buildings they now owned. They could hear every word of the argument.

"Should we interfere?" Paul asked.

"No," Candy said, shaking her head. "Let's let them see if they can figure this out. We can't move them for several months yet, so they'll have to live together up there for a while. Bailey seems to be the calmest and most levelheaded of the three, though. Grant did well when he hired her."

"I agree," Paul said. "She's a jewel, especially for a kid right out of college with no work experience."

Candy giggled. "I remember when you made a wrong choice in that department."

Paul rolled his eyes, "Don't remind me." The Garners turned their attention to the engineer who was pointing to the wall.

Grant walked up the hallway to Bailey's desk.

"I don't appreciate the ear plug comment," he said.

Bailey looked at him and said, "I had to do something to get you two to lower your voices and quit arguing. Paul and Candy are on the second floor with an engineer, and they could hear everything you were saying. Heck, the diners in the café could probably hear you."

"How do you know they're on the second floor?" Grant asked.

"I heard their conversation from the floor below," she replied pointing downward. "That's how I know they could hear yours."

Realizing she was right annoyed Grant even more. The last thing he wanted was to look bad in front of his employer. Frustrated, Grant returned to his office.

Later in the morning, Kelli descended the back stairs and entered the first floor hallway just as Candy was coming out of the bakery.

"Hey," Candy said. "Is everything okay?"

"It's fine," Kelli replied. "I'm on my way to see Tracy. I have an appointment this afternoon to discuss a menu with a bride-to-be whose reception is in two months. I was going to get a list of foods and prices to show her. I'm sure you have one, but availability and costs change, so I thought I would get an update."

"What's the date?" Candy asked. "Let me see if I'm doing the cake."

They walked back to Candy's office to check her calendar where Kelli gave her the date.

"Yes," Candy said. "I'm making the cake. The bride is Deena Hicks. Her mother teaches at the high school. Tell Tracy the cake is white with a few light pink flowers. If the bride wants punch, Tracy usually tries to make it match."

"That gives me an idea," Kelli said. "I'm going to walk down the street to the florist and see if they're doing the wedding. Maybe I can get an idea of the flowers and colors. It never hurts to have extra information."

Candy smiled. "Agreed."

Grant felt his stomach growl. He looked at the clock on his computer and realized it was almost one o'clock. No wonder he was hungry. He closed out the program he was working on and turned off his computer. Walking down the hall, he saw that Bailey was gone. She had told him she needed to leave for a couple hours early this afternoon and that she would trade them for her on-call tonight.

The café was his only option for lunch since he needed to go grocery shopping after work. The humid summer heat hit him in the face when he walked out the door to cross the street, which made the café's air conditioning a welcome relief as he took a seat on a stool at the counter.

After giving his order to the waitress, Grant looked around the room. His eyes stopped at Tracy's office. Oh, this is just great. He needed lunch, and Kelli was sitting in Tracy's office. He couldn't seem get away from the woman. Grant got the waitress's attention and asked for his meal to be changed to a takeout. He could eat in peace upstairs.

"Thanks, Tracy," Kelli said as she stood. "You've helped a lot. I now know what to offer and how much it costs."

"You're welcome," Tracy said. "You may as well get lunch while you're here. Candy charges employees half price. We can't eat for free because of the costs, but it's still a nice perk."

"A very nice perk," Kelli said as she looked out at the dining room. The only seat available was a stool at the counter where Grant was sitting. Kelli took a deep breath and placed a smile on her face.

"Hello, Grant," she said as she sat down. "I see we had the same idea for lunch."

"I guess," he answered. The waitress brought Grant's meal. He got up, paid his bill and left the café through the back entrance.

"What put his panties in a wad?" Tracy asked. "I've never seen the guy rude before, and we've been friends for a long time."

"Me." Kelli said. "He hates me."

"That doesn't sound like Grant," Tracy said sounding confused. "Why would he hate you?"

"There was a vacant office on the third floor between him and Bailey. Candy and Paul put me in it. He's not happy about that," Kelli explained. "He says I'm loud and that I keep him and Bailey from concentrating. We got into a big argument this morning. He's still mad."

"Grant?" Tracy exclaimed incredulously. "What in the world? He's usually the epitome of patience, rational thought and common sense. You must have hit the one nerve he has."

"I guess," Kelli said, sighing. "I'm wondering if he's mad because he wanted to move Bailey into that office. Is he territorial?"

"I've never known him to be," Tracy said as she reached for an order pad. "This is a mystery to me. What do you want to eat?"

Kelli ordered a grilled chicken salad and water. She considered getting it to go, but decided eating there was just easier. It worked out well because she had a chance to talk with Tracy while she ate. Kelli liked her and hoped they would be friends.

Grant looked out the window of his apartment as he ate his lunch. It was peaceful and quiet up here. He wished the offices across the street had as much sound insulation as this apartment did. It was busy in the café, but he couldn't hear any of it. After he finished eating, Grant wished he had brought his laptop with him. He could have worked from here. He sighed. It looked like he would be going back to the office with Miss Kelli Loudmouth.

While he was staring out the window, Kelli left the café and walked back across the street. Grant watched her. Her hair was in its customary ponytail, but she looked nice in the summer dress that lightly hugged her hips as she walked. The woman was attractive, he would give her that. If she weren't so annoying, it might be nice to get to know her.

The afternoon was quieter than the morning. Grant was pleased with that. When the phone was not ringing, he couldn't tell Kelli was even on the floor. Wanting air flow, Grant decided to open his office door.

Around four, the elevator opened, and Grant saw two women enter the lobby. They approached Bailey and asked where Kelli's office was. Bailey didn't look up; she just pointed down the hall. Grant flew angry all over again. He had told Paul he didn't want Bailey to act as a receptionist or hostess for Kelli, and here she was, being forced to do that on Kelli's second week at work.

The women found Kelli. Grant rolled his eyes as they ooh'd and aah'd over choices of food for the menu. He literally squirmed when one of the women let out a high pitch giggle. When he could take it no longer, Grant closed his laptop. He picked it up, collected his input data, and walked down the hall. He stopped at Bailey's desk.

"Are you having trouble concentrating?" he asked quietly.

"Why would I be having trouble concentrating?" she asked, looking confused.

Grant looked at her in disbelief. He pointed down the hall and said, "That noise in the other office."

Bailey looked around and said, "I hadn't noticed. I was concentrating on these schedules." She pointed to her computer screen, "Look at this gap in freight service. Someone could do well opening a trucking company in that area. Didn't Paul used to be a truck driver? Maybe he could do that."

Grant looked at the map she was showing him.

"Can you print that graphic?" he asked. Bailey nodded, punched the keys and the map came out of the printer.

"Thanks," he said. "I'm going to show this to Paul. I'll give you the credit for noticing, then it will be up to him to decide what to do."

Grant took out his phone and called Paul.

"Hey, Paul," he said, "are you in the building?"

"No," Paul replied. "I'm working from home this afternoon. Is everything okay?"

"Everything's fine," Grant replied, "but Bailey found something interesting. There's a gap in freight service between some of our vendors. I'll have her send you the graphic. Maybe you can get someone to put a trucking company out there." He whispered to Bailey to email the map to Paul.

"Do you have the sales data for last month?" Paul asked.

"I'm almost finished with the data input," Grant replied. "I'll have the reports to you in about an hour."

"Are you at the office?" Paul asked.

"Yes, I'm here, but I'm leaving," Grant replied. "I need to go to the apartment to finish. It's quieter there."

"All right, I'll see you in the morning," Paul said.

As Paul ended the call, he was worried. It wasn't like Grant to have so much trouble adjusting to a new situation. He hoped Grant and Kelli could get to know each other and tolerate working in adjoining offices. If not, both his and Candy's businesses could suffer.

Kelli was extremely pleased with how the appointment with the bride had gone. Deena and her mother had been happy with the setup of the hall, the decorations, the food, and the cake. The groom's family had also booked the second floor for the rehearsal dinner. The mother of the groom had an appointment on Thursday to choose the dinner menu. She assumed Candy was making a groom's cake, but she would find out. Overall, except for the argument with Grant, it had been a good day.

CHAPTER 7

Thursday morning, Kelli dressed in shorts and a t-shirt before going to the office. Her goal was to look through the basement. She wanted to know exactly what was there, compare it to Candy's inventory, and see if there needed to be any rearrangement of the items.

Kelli waved at Candy as she came through the back door. She went up the stairs to the third floor and put her computer on her desk. After placing a suit bag with business clothes on the hook behind her door, Kelli walked back down the stairs to the basement.

Looking around the room, Kelli started by taking vases, candlesticks, napkins, and tablecloths out of one cabinet. She listed the items and counted them, registering the totals in a notebook.

Kelli was concentrating on her job so hard, she lost track of time. She heard the growling in her stomach before she felt it. Looking at her watch, she gasped in surprise. It was almost one o'clock. Her appointment with Mrs. Blalock was at fifteen minutes after one. She dropped the linen napkins that were in her hands and ran up the stairs to the first floor. Ellen handed her a piece of the vegetable quiche and a cup of tea in to-go containers.

The elevator opened on the third floor, and Kelli awkwardly balanced her food as she ran down the hall to her office. Closing the door, she took her business clothes out of the suit bag and laid them across her chair. Kelli took a bite of quiche and a gulp of tea. Her phone rang; it was Candy.

Kelli answered, "Hey, let me put you on speaker. I need both hands right now."

"What are you doing?" Candy asked.

"I'm trying to eat, change clothes, brush my hair and get ready for Mrs. Blalock's appointment in fifteen minutes," Kellis said breathlessly. "Time slipped up on me while I was working in the basement."

Candy laughed, "I was just going to give you the theme and colors for the groom's cake the Blalock's asked for. It's baseball and the colors are red, white and blue."

"Sounds fun," Kelli said. "What's the groom's connection to baseball?"

"He played minor league baseball, and now he's going to coach at the high school next spring," Candy answered.

"Ah, makes sense," Kelli said. She took another bite of quiche and pulled her shirt over her head. Looking in a mirror, she checked her face, arms and hair for dirt or cobwebs as she stepped out of her shorts.

The morning had been peaceful, just like Grant liked it, but he was startled when he heard the phone ring and Kelli answered. Then he realized he was listening to both sides of the conversation. She had the call on speaker! He couldn't believe she would do that after she had promised to keep things quieter. Grant felt anger flush through his body. He got up and stormed out of his office to Kelli's. He didn't bother to knock.

He pushed the door open and said angrily, "Can you never be quiet? Now you have calls on speaker?"

Kelli looked up in shock, then she was angry.

"Don't you knock?" she yelled.

Grant halted in his steps. Kelli was standing behind her desk in her underwear. He saw the the pile of dusty clothes on the floor and the clean clothes draped across her chair. He had no words. He closed the door and walked back to his office. He felt terrible.

"What happened?" Candy asked. "What's going on?"

"It's nothing," Kelli said. "Grant was momentarily angry that we were talking too loudly and reminded me that I had promised to be quieter and less disruptive. Look, Candy, can I call you back after this appointment? I need to get changed and clean up my mess in here."

"Sure. We'll talk later," Candy said and ended the call.

Kelli quickly changed into a summer dress and sandals. She finished the quiche and had just enough time to straighten her office and brush her teeth in the bathroom. At exactly 1:15, Kelli calmly greeted Mrs. Blalock and asked her to have a seat.

The mother of the groom was pleased with the plans for the groom's cake. She chose a menu and asked for a royal blue color scheme. With everything approved, Kelli took the woman's check for the down payment and escorted her to the elevator.

"I'll ride down with you," Kelli said. "I need to see Candy in the bakery."

Kelli watched Mrs. Blalock leave the building then she

went into the bakery looking for Candy. Kelli found her in the kitchen piping pink frosting on a princess birthday cake.

"Let me guess," Kellie said, "a little girl's birthday cake."

Candy laughed, "That would be correct." When Kelli held up the check, Candy said, "Put it on my desk if you don't mind. I've got my hands full right now."

Kelli put the check where Candy requested and went back into the kitchen.

"Mrs. Blalock loved the baseball themed groom's cake," Kelli told her, "and she's matching the icing with a royal blue color scheme."

Candy smiled, "I thought she would like that. Now, tell me who didn't knock when we were talking."

"Oh, it was just Grant blowing off steam again," Kelli said. "When I made the knocking remark, he seemed to realize he had been rude. He retreated and didn't push the issue. It's no big deal, honestly."

Kelli watched Candy switch to making tiny frosting daisies then said, "In fairness to him, I was on speaker, and it sounded loud even to me. We'll work it out; don't worry. If I had paid more attention to the time, I wouldn't have been in a tizzy trying to get ready. So, it's partly my fault."

"I need to get back," Kelli said. As she was leaving the kitchen she said, "Oh, by the way, that quiche is delicious. You should put a sign out when you make it and sell whole ones."

"I'll think about that," Candy said as she looked up at Kelli and smiled. "I'm glad you liked it."

Kelli rode the elevator back up to the third floor. She got off the elevator and was glad to see that Bailey did not acknowledge her but kept on working. Kelli grinned as she walked by Bailey's desk. That girl could tune out a rock band, sirens, and a pipe organ all sounding at the same time.

As Kelli walked back into her office and closed her door, she looked at her watch and saw that it was three o'clock. What an afternoon it had been. Kelli rested her head back on her chair, suddenly exhausted. The tension with Grant had finally gotten to her. Tomorrow she would try working from the basement. If her phone had a good signal, she could just set up shop down there. It wasn't an uncomfortable space, and there were even tables and chairs she could use.

Kelli took a deep breath and let it out. She took a sip of the sweet tea and opened her computer. She had started a social media page and a website for the bakery, catering and events company. She wanted to link them to a message board where people could ask questions in private. She was having difficulty linking the sites to the message application when a knock sounded on her door.

"Come in." she answered without looking up.

Grant walked in and sat in the chair across from her. Kelli heard heavy footsteps and looked up. She was surprised, because she thought it was Candy at the door.

Kelli squinted her eyes at him thoughtfully then said, "You are just the man I need right now."

"Excuse me?" Grant asked with raised eyebrows.

"Look at this," she said, turning her laptop around to him. "I need to link a website and a social media page to this application to receive and send messages. I cannot for the life of me get it to work. Can you figure out what I'm doing wrong?"

Grant slid the laptop closer to him and scrolled through the website and social media page. From her side of the desk, Kelli watched as he concentrated on the screen and punched a few buttons.

"That should do it," Grant said as he turned the laptop back around to Kelli. "It wasn't your fault. For some reason the application was freezing up. I just entered them differently."

Kelli looked at the two sites and tested the message app.

"Thanks!" she said with a smile. "You're my hero today. Now, what can I do for you?"

"I came to apologize," he said. "I had no right to barge in here without knocking. I'm especially sorry I caught you in an awkward situation." He wanted to tell her she was beautiful, but that would be inappropriate and pushing his luck.

"Yes, you should have knocked," Kelli said with a firm nod of her head, "but I'll admit it was loud, and I'm sorry for that. I lost track of time and had only a few minutes to get everything done before my client arrived. I put Candy on the speaker so I could multitask. I don't plan to make a habit of changing clothes in here. I would have gone to the restroom, but I didn't have time."

"Well, I'm sorry," Grant said. "I hope I didn't embarrass you."

Kelli waved her hand dismissively, "I have bikinis that show more. No big deal. It's the fact that it was underwear that makes it feel awkward."

"Did Candy ask you about it?" he asked. "You were on speaker."

"Yes, but I blew it off," Kelli answered. "I told her I was

in the wrong this time and you were letting me know. Don't worry about it. Besides, I think I've come up with a solution. I'll work more hours in the basement. There's a table and some chairs there, so if the cell phone and Wi-Fi reception are good, I can work down there except for appointments."

Now Grant really did feel bad. He had succeeded in getting her off the third floor, but he wasn't feeling like a winner. He was feeling like a jerk.

"Don't feel like you have to do that," he said.

Kelli rolled her eyes. "You and I both know that my staying up here is always going to be a thorn in your side. Just because you saw me in a bra and panties does not mean you have to do or say something you don't mean."

She grinned, "Just tell Paul you want the third floor of the next building. They will be connecting it to this one so the same elevator can service both buildings. There will be a thick glass wall and door where the brick used to be. Put some extra sound proofing in your offices and you'll be fine." She broadened her grin and winked, "Then I can have this floor and your office, which is great I might add."

Grant was floored. She was acting like nothing had happened. She had even waved off his apology like it was unnecessary and taken the blame for his being upset. But that grin and wink, now that got his attention.

"Thanks for being so understanding," Grant said as he stood. He was full of conflicting emotions, and guilt was high on the list. "Again, I'm sorry for barging in on you."

"Thanks for fixing my messaging problem," Kelli said. "Hey, when I finish the website and social media page, will you take a look at them and see how I can improve?"

"Sure. Anytime," he answered and left the room.

Kelli smiled to herself; computer problems solved. Remembering she wanted pictures for the website, Kelli got up and went downstairs to get a picture of that cute princess cake.

Candy was just getting ready to do the writing on the cake when Kelli came in.

"Have you written a name on the cake yet?" Kelli asked.

"No," Candy answered. "Why?"

"I want a picture of it with no name. I'm going to put it online," Kelli answered and started to take pictures with her phone.

"Online?" Candy asked.

"Yes. You now have a website and a social media page for the bakery and events business. Both are linked to a private messaging application. Grant helped me connect both to the messaging. People can ask questions online. That should reduce phone calls, which will make him happy."

"I now have a social media page and a website?" Candy asked. "When did that happen?"

"I started them a few days ago, and I'm working on them today. They're a work in progress, though." Kelli pulled the website up on her phone. "See, it's pretty basic. A picture of the building, the bakery display case, the buffet spread from Saturday night and in a few minutes your cute princess cake will be on it." Kelli continued scrolling through the website, showing Candy its contents.

"I am going to get permission from couples to use their picture cutting their wedding cake that you make," Kelli said. "I will post pictures of the tables, decorations, venue setup. They will be accessible from the website menu under headings like cakes, events, catering, and whatever else I can come up with."

"This is fantastic, Kelli. I never thought about doing this," Candy said.

"You're still growing. At first you were local and got business by word of mouth. Now you're getting busier, and this will help you grow even more." She looked at Candy, "You need a few bed and breakfast houses and a chapel. Then you could be a wedding destination."

Candy laughed, "I'm not sure I want to get that involved. Just receptions and cakes for now."

Kelli turned to leave, "Think about it. Paul and his brother could make some sweet B & Bs."

Candy laughed as she watched Kelli leave the kitchen.

CHAPTER 8

<hr>

True to her words, Kelli had spent the next week working in the basement more often. The disadvantage was that her calendars and all the paperwork were on the third floor. It was only mid-morning, and she had already dropped what she was doing to go back up the stairs three times to get information from the filing cabinet.

Grant heard Kelli walk down the hall, again. How many times had this been, four? He had just settled back into his task when the phone rang.

"Cotton Catering and Events." Grant thought if he never heard that greeting again, it would be too soon.

Sighing in frustration, Grant leaned back in his chair and closed his eyes. This was Wednesday, and the phone was as busy as a Monday. If she did not get off that blasted phone soon, he was going to have to go back to his apartment to work, but he didn't want to do that. Since Kelli had started, Paul had come to the office twice looking for him only to find that he had gone home.

Grant heard a different phone ring tone.

"Hey!" Kelly answered. "What's up?"

Grant assumed it was her private cell phone. He heard Kelli talking with what sounded like an old work colleague. Every word came through the wall loud and clear. It sounded like Kelli was teaching someone to do a job long distance.

After a few long minutes of listening to what seemed to be a very detailed conversation, Grant angrily slammed his laptop shut. He decided that if Kelli wasn't going to work in the basement, then he would. He stormed down the hall, passed Bailey without speaking, and got on the elevator. He angrily pushed the button for the lower level.

Grant got off the elevator in the basement. The lights were still on over the entire space. Grant looked around. He had never been to the basement before. He found the table and chairs where it appeared Kelli had been working and put his laptop down. Fascinated, Grant began to walk through the paths of items used for every kind of event imaginable.

The cabinets were all open displaying the varied colors of tablecloths, chair covers, candles, and candle holders. Wooden folding chairs were stacked along one wall. Rolls of fabrics were placed in holders making one entire wall a burst of color. At first glance, the room looked like chaos, but he could see the beginning of order. Grant was impressed with Kelli's organizational skills.

Kelli finished her call then found the information she wanted. She noticed that the samples she had brought up for an appointment the day before were still in the office and decided to take them with her back to the basement. Juggling papers, fabrics and a tall candlestick,

Kelli used the stairs to return to the basement. Entering the room, she walked toward her table and was startled to see the silhouette of a man standing in the shadows of a cabinet with his back to her. He was looking into one of the cabinets and holding a vase. She screamed, dropped her fabrics and papers, and swung the brass candlestick.

Grant was admiring some of the vases and dishes in one of the cabinets. He didn't hear the basement door open. He jumped in surprise when he heard a woman scream. Then he felt a searing pain as something hit him on the head. The blow made him dizzy and sent him to his knees for a moment.

Kelli hit the man in the head. She dropped the candlestick and heard it clatter on the floor as she ran back up the stairs. She came out onto the first floor, ran into the bakery and told Ellen to call the police. There was a strange man in the basement, and he had the cabinets open, taking out the contents.

Candy ran out of the kitchen when she heard an obviously distressed Kelli telling Ellen to call the police.

"What's going on?" she asked.

"There's a strange man in the basement!" Kelli exclaimed as she paced the sitting area of the bakery. She faced Candy and ran a trembling hand through her hair.

"He had one of the cabinets open and was taking stuff out of it," she said. "I was startled and screamed. I dropped everything I had in my hands but the candleholder. Then, on pure reflex, I hit the man with it. I saw him drop to his knees before I turned and ran back up the stairs. He's still down there. I haven't seen him come up the stairs or the elevator, and there's no other way out."

Candy could see Kelli had been frightened, but that she was beginning to calm down.

"Paul is the only man that would have any business in the basement, and he's out of town," Candy said with a worried frown and made Kelli sit at one of the tables. Just then Officer Hank Bowen calmly walked through the door.

"Hey Candy," he said. "Ellen said you have an intruder in the basement."

"Hello Hank," Candy said. She pointed to Kelli. "Evidently, Kelli went into the basement and found a strange man taking a vase out of one of the cabinets. She screamed and hit him with the candlestick she had in her hand."

Hank turned to Kelli, "Is that how it happened?"

"Yes," Kelli told the officer. "That is exactly what happened. Also, I was so scared I dropped everything I was carrying. It's all over the floor."

Hank looked at Candy, "How do I get into the basement?"

"The elevator or the back stairs. Either one will get you there," Candy answered. "Plus, those are the only two ways out of the basement. He couldn't leave without us seeing him."

"Show me the stairs," Hank said.

Candy showed Hank the door to the stairwell, and Hank quietly descended to the basement.

Grant felt something running down his head into the back of his shirt. He put his hand on the back of his head and felt a sticky wetness. Grant looked at his hand which was now covered in blood and grabbed the first piece of cloth available which was a white linen napkin. When he tried to stand, the room started spinning, making him nauseous. Grant stumbled to a chair. He sat and pressed the napkin to the back of his head, closed his eyes and wondered if this day could get any worse. But it did.

Grant heard, "Put your hands up where I can see them."

Oh great. That sounded like Officer Hank. The woman had actually called the police on him.

Grant raised one hand and said, "If I raise the other one, I will bleed all over the chair and everything else down here."

"Who are you?" Hank asked.

"I'm Grant Sparks," he said, fumbling for his wallet and identification. "I work on the third floor for Paul Garner and Garner Logistics. It was so noisy up there that I decided to work down here, hoping it was quiet. I didn't know I was going to be assaulted."

Hank came around the table and looked at him. A look of understanding and relief was visible in his eyes.

"Are you hurt?" he asked.

"Apparently. The shrew hit me with a candlestick." Grant pointed to the weapon lying on the floor. The end was covered with blood and Grant's hair.

"Shrew?" Hank asked, eyebrows raised.

"Yes, Shrew," Grant answered angrily. "Kelli Mills. She has a voice like a shrew, always on loud. She was supposed to work down here today, but she decided to go up to the third floor and take her phone calls. The woman has no volume button."

Hank looked at Grant, who was pale and bleeding. After putting on a pair of gloves, Hank tipped Grant's head slightly to look at the wound.

"I think we need to get you to a doctor," Hank said. "I'll be glad to take you to the urgent care on the other side of town. I don't think you should be driving."

Grant looked at the napkin that was almost completely red with blood.

He picked up another one and said, "Maybe I'd better go. I think I may need a stitch or two to stop this bleeding. My head hurts like she used a sledgehammer instead of a candleholder. That woman is strong."

"Can you stand?" Hank asked.

"I tried to at first, but the room kept spinning. It may be better now." Grant stood. The room started to spin again, and he sat back down.

Hank got on his radio and called the dispatcher.

"Emma, can you send an ambulance to the bakery. Tell them to come down the elevator to the basement. I have a head injury here, and he can't stand without the room spinning."

"Don't try to stand, Grant," Hank ordered. "You may have a concussion. I think you need the emergency room instead of urgent care."

Grant continued to press the napkin against his head and said, "I'm in no shape to argue."

Kelli looked at Candy, "What's taking him so long?"

"I don't know," Candy replied, "but Hank is very good at his job. Don't worry."

Candy and Kelli looked surprised when an ambulance drove up and two EMTs brought a stretcher inside.

"What's going on?" Candy asked them.

"Hank called and said he had a head wound in your

basement," the medic answered as he pushed the elevator button.

Candy looked at Kelli who was looking worried.

"Kelli, stay here with Ellen," Candy said. "I'm going downstairs with them. It's my basement. I need to see what's happening."

Candy got on the elevator with the EMTs. When the doors opened, she saw Hank standing over a man who was sitting on a chair holding his head with one of her linen napkins. Another napkin lay on the table, and it was soaked with blood.

The EMTs approached the man and started their assessment. Candy still couldn't see who it was.

Hank walked over to her and said, "I think we have a case of mistaken identity. That's Grant Sparks from your third floor. He showed me his ID."

"Grant!" she exclaimed. "What's he doing down here?"

"Evidently the woman he called a shrew was so loud he couldn't work and decided to come down here where she was supposed to be working. He said he was just trying to find a quiet place to work. He had his back to the stairs when she returned. The incident with the vase was that he was admiring your inventory. He liked your style," Hank explained.

Candy gasped and put a hand over her mouth. The EMTs had Grant on the stretcher and were rolling him toward the elevator.

She walked over to him and asked, "Grant, are you all right?"

"I will be as soon as the bleeding stops, the room stops spinning and the headache goes away," he replied. Before the elevator doors opened Grant pointed to the candlestick and said to Hank, "Officer, that candlestick is evidence. I suggest you take care of it."

Hank put on gloves and pulled a plastic bag from a pouch on his belt. He picked up the candlestick and placed it inside the bag before sealing it.

Kelli was watching the elevator. She was still trembling and felt a tightness in her chest. She didn't think she had hit the man that hard, but she had been so scared in the moment that she acted instinctively. Besides, what was he doing down there in the first place?

The elevator opened. The EMT's came out with the stretcher. The man was lying back, holding a bloody napkin to his head. It hid his face from her view. Candy and Hank came out of the elevator behind the stretcher.

Candy walked over to Kelli and said, "Kelli, it was Grant. He had gone down there to work because he said he couldn't work upstairs."

A look of horror came across Kelli's face.

"What? I hit Grant?" she asked.

"Yes. He needs stitches and may have a concussion," Candy informed her.

"I didn't know!" she exclaimed as tears filled her eyes. The stretcher was almost to the door that opened to the street. Kelli ran to catch up with it.

"Grant, I didn't know it was you!" she said. "I'm so sorry."

Kelli saw Grant grimace as he tried to move his head.

"I don't want to talk to you right now," Grant snarled as he looked at Kelli out of one eye. "Stay away from me."

Kelli felt tears in her eye, "But Grant, I'm so sorry."

The EMTs had stopped, and Grant said to them, "Can we go, please?"

Kelli watched them put Grant into the ambulance. Tears were streaming down her face. Candy came up beside her.

"Paul is out of town, but he's on his way back. I'm going to the emergency room. Ellen will watch the bakery," Candy said.

"I didn't know it was Grant," Kelli cried. "I was so shocked and scared that I had walked into a burglary. I feel terrible!"

"I know," Candy said. "It's an unfortunate incident. We'll have to straighten it out. Can you tell me why he would have left the third floor?"

"I don't know," Kelli said. "I just answered two calls, one on the business phone and one on my phone. The one on my phone was lengthy because I was trying to explain a procedure to the girl who took my place at my last job. I didn't think I was talking too loudly, and my door was closed. But Grant has very little tolerance for anything I do upstairs. I could have whispered, and it would have bothered him."

Kelli paused, then said, "Candy, I will rearrange the basement and make an office space down there until all the renovations are finished. Then you and Paul can decide where you want us."

"I know you feel bad," Candy said. "The flip side to this is if it had really been a burglar, you would be a hero right now instead of feeling like you did the worst thing in the world. Remember that. We'll get this worked out." Candy left the bakery, got in her car and followed the ambulance to the hospital.

Kelli took the elevator back to the third floor. She passed Bailey who never looked up. She walked to her office, closed the door and cried.

*****

Grant was miserable. His head hurt, and he couldn't have any pain meds until he had a CT scan.

"Grant?"

Grant heard Candy's voice at the door of his room in the hospital's emergency department.

"Yes," he answered without opening his eyes.

"Do you need anything?" she asked.

"No," he said flatly.

"Paul is on his way back into town. He'll be here as soon as he can," she said.

"Tell him not to change his schedule. I'll live," Grant said.

"He's concerned," Candy said. "We all are."

Grant said, "If you don't mind, could you find my cell phone and bring it to me? It's somewhere in the basement, probably on the table where I left my computer. I may need to call my family."

"Of course. I'll do that right now," Candy said. "I'll be back as soon as I can." Grant had never opened his eyes. Candy looked at him with concern then left the room.

CHAPTER 9

Across town, Kelli was miserable. She wished she had never gone back to the basement or had never gone up to the third floor. Either way would have been better than this. Having Grant yell at her was better than this. Arguing with Grant was better than this. Three weeks on the job and she had almost killed a coworker. She wondered if she should start looking for another job. Candy had every right to fire her over this incident.

Kelli sighed, got up and took the stairs to the basement. She picked up the papers and samples that she had dropped on the floor. Going over to the table she saw a linen napkin soaked with blood. That needed to be cleaned up.

Boxes of serving gloves and trash bags for catering events were stored in a corner. Kelli put on a pair of gloves and took an extra one to the table. She stuffed the napkin into the extra glove and double-bagged it with the gloves from her hands. She put on more gloves, got a disinfectant wipe and cleaned the table. She looked at the floor. There was only one drop of blood, and she cleaned that up.

Grant's cell phone and computer were sitting on the table. Kelli picked them up and wondered if she should take them to the hospital when Candy came into the room from the elevator.

Looking at Candy, Kelli asked, "How is he?"

Candy could see Kelli had been crying. She knew the woman felt terrible.

"I don't know," she said. "He's waiting on a CT scan. He can't have pain meds until they make a diagnosis, and his headache is severe. He asked me to come get his cell phone. I'm going to take his laptop up to his office for safekeeping."

"I can take the laptop and save you a trip," Kelli said. "Candy, I feel terrible. I never meant to hurt Grant. I thought there was a burglar in here."

"I know that," Candy said, looking at Kelli with compassion, "and in time, Grant will remember that. He's just in too much discomfort right now to be rational about it."

"I cleaned up in here," Kelli said and pointed to the pile of disinfectant wipes, "but I can't find the candlestick. I need to clean it and put it away."

Candy winced, "Hank took it. He bagged it as evidence."

Kelli looked at Candy with horror.

"Evidence! As in a crime? I had no intention of hurting Grant!" she exclaimed. Kelli started to cry again.

"Don't borrow trouble," Candy said as she placed a hand on Kelli's shoulder. "Hank wasn't going to do that until Grant pointed to it and told him to. Grant was angry at the time. I don't think he will do anything about it."

"I'm so sorry," Kelli said miserably. "I would never hurt Grant on purpose." She sat in the chair, put her head in her arms on the table and sobbed.

Candy sat beside Kelli and put her arm around her.

"I know, Kelli. We all know you would never hurt him or anyone else. It was just an extremely unfortunate event." Candy sighed and picked up Grant's cellphone. "I need to get this to Grant. He wants to call his family."

Kelli sat up and wiped her eyes, "Of course. Go. Take care of him. I'll get the laptop upstairs."

Kelli watched Candy get back on the elevator with Grant's phone. She picked up the soiled napkin inside the gloves, and the dirty cleaning supplies. She took them to the kitchen and threw them in the large garbage container.

Kelli returned to the basement and got Grant's laptop. She climbed the stairs to the third floor. She stepped out into the hallway and walked around Bailey's desk to Grant's office. After placing the laptop on his desk, Kelli went back to her office and started packing things up.

The calendars and office supplies were the first to be taken back down the stairs. She rode up the elevator with a hand truck which she used to move the filing cabinet downstairs. Going back up the stairs, Kelli surveyed her now empty office. The desk and chairs were all that was left. Kelli moved the Ficus tree to the windows in Grant's office and watered it.

In the basement Kelli rearranged the tables to make an L shaped desk with her filing cabinet behind it. There were wooden folding chairs she would use if she brought someone downstairs. Kelli's stomach growled. It was two in the afternoon. She went upstairs, got a piece of quiche and a tea then brought them back to the basement. It was windowless, dark and drab, but she would get used to it. She couldn't afford another mistake with Grant.

Grant's CT scan showed a very short, very mild linear fracture on his skull. The doctors told him that it would heal on its own and put two stitches in his scalp. Candy brought Grant's phone to him and told him she was going to wait for Paul who was almost there. Grant told Candy his diagnosis and that he had been given two acetaminophen tablets which were already helping ease the throbbing in his skull.

Grant called his parents who said they would be there as soon as they could. The doctor had asked him not to stay alone for the next 24 hours. Also, no computer time for 48 hours and then to phase it back in gradually. Grant was not happy with those instructions, but he agreed to follow them.

Paul entered Grant's room just as Grant's parents were getting to the hospital. He told Grant to get well and not worry about the job.

"I'll take care of your end until you're back. After all, I did it before you did," Paul said with a grin.

"I know," Grant said, ginning back at Paul, "but I don't want you to think you can live without me. I like this job."

"No chance of that, buddy," Paul said with a chuckle. "I need you too much."

"Your laptop is on your desk, safe and sound," Candy assured Grant. "Paul can use it if he needs to. You just get better, and don't rush the recovery."

Candy and Paul met Grant's parents and exchanged polite greetings. Paul assured them that Grant would be given as much time as he needed to fully recuperate.

Once they were back in the hospital lobby, Paul said, "Let's go get some food. I want to go out toward the interstate where we can talk. I need you to give me details on what happened."

Over a late afternoon pizza, Candy told Paul exactly what she had seen and what she had been told by Kelli, Grant, and Officer Hank. She gave him the reasons Grant was in the basement, and she told him how bad Kelli felt.

"Are you going to let her keep her job?" Paul asked before taking a bite of pizza.

"Of course," Candy said frowning as she wiped her fingers on a napkin. "Why wouldn't I? She would have never hurt Grant on purpose. You know that as well as I do. She thought she was stopping a burglary. Why should I make matters worse by letting her go, especially when she's proving to be so very good at her job?"

"You're right, I guess," Paul said. "But what do we do about the work situation between those two? I can't lose Paul, and you can't lose Kelli."

Candy took a sip of her drink and said, "If I'm right, when I get back to the bakery, Kelli will have moved her office to the basement. She had planned to work there today. It was just a coincidence that she took a phone call upstairs while she was there looking for paperwork. Kelli is trying to make this right, but Grant is not innocent in this. For some reason he overreacts where Kelli is concerned. Bailey has no problems with her, even likes her. But Kelli can't seem to do anything right as far as Grant is concerned."

"You're right," Paul said. "We can let Kelli have the basement until this all blows over. When the third floor is finished in the other building, I can move Paul and Bailey over there. Remind me to have Chip put in extra insulation or whatever he uses to soundproof the offices. I've done this job. It can get intense, and I know how frustrating it can be to lose your focus just as you're getting ready to figure out the puzzle."

"I understand that," Candy said, "but Kelli's personality is perfect for her job. She needs to be bubbly, informative, and helpful. She can't do that without talking. I've heard her, and I don't think she's as loud as Grant complains that she is. He's just overly sensitive where she's concerned."

Paul grinned, "Like you used to be about me."

Candy laughed, almost choking on a piece of pizza.

"Don't remind me," she said then stopped and looked at Paul. "You don't think there's potential for a relationship there, do you?"

Paul shrugged, "Stranger things have happened. Look at us!"

Candy chuckled and took another bite of pizza. The subject changed to more mundane subjects as the two discussed their businesses.

CHAPTER 10

G rant sat on his parents' back porch watching the birds fuss with each other over seeds at the bird feeder. He found that out here he could escape his mother's hovering. She was constantly asking how he was or offering him something to eat. He appreciated their concern, but he was getting tired of the attention.

Most of all, Grant was bored. He couldn't work, he couldn't watch TV, and he couldn't read. Plus his head hurt. Even with acetaminophen, the pain was still there. However, he had made it 24 hours. He could go home. Sitting on his own balcony watching Whitlow would be better than bird watching.

That night Grant sighed with pleasure when his body laid down on his own bed. His parents had wanted him to stay another night with them, but finally agreed to take him back to Whitlow when he threatened to call a taxi. Grant understood their concern, but he wanted his own place, his own bed, and his own space. All he had to do was make it to lunch tomorrow and he could ease himself back into work.

Friday morning, a hot shower and a cup of coffee

worked wonders. Grant felt better than he had in two days, and his headache was almost gone. He walked downstairs to the café and ordered an egg biscuit to go.

It was still cool enough that Grant drank his coffee and ate his biscuit on the balcony. He looked down into the bakery windows. A flash of color caught his eye, and he saw Kelli walk through the bakery sitting area. She had on a red summer dress. She must have an appointment later. Well, it wouldn't matter if they were loud. He wasn't there to hear it.

He had been so angry at Kelli. If she had just stopped a moment, she would have seen that it was him and not an intruder. Or maybe she saw him as an intruder in her space, he didn't know. He felt bad about telling Hank Bowen to bag the evidence. He really didn't need to do that, but he wished he could have seen Kelli's expression when she found that out.

Grant watched Candy come out of the bakery and walk across the street to the café. She was carrying a box with the bakery's logo. She looked up, saw him, smiled, and waved. He waved back.

While he was sitting there wondering why Kelli was taking bakery goods to the cafe, Grant heard his phone ring. Realizing he had left it inside, Grant walked back into the apartment to answer it. It was Paul.

"Hey Paul," Grant answered.

"Grant," Paul said, "glad you're back at the apartment. Try watching TV in spurts this afternoon. If you can do that without any headache or other bad effects, let me know and I'll get your computer to you tomorrow."

"Okay," Grant said, even though he was a little disappointed that he couldn't get the computer today. "That sounds like a plan. I'll see you tomorrow."

He was just about to go back to the balcony when Grant heard a knock at his door. He opened it. Tracy stood there with a bakery box.

"This is for you," she said and handed him the box.

"Thanks," he said as he watched her hurry back down the stairs. Going back to the kitchen, he placed the box on the island. Inside was a cheese Danish and a card. It was a get-well card. The note at the bottom said, *I am so sorry, Kelli.*

Grant had a momentary flash of anger, but it was quickly gone. He knew Kelli had to feel horrible about what happened. He also knew that if he had not over-reacted to her phone calls, he would never have gone to the basement. She had no way of knowing he was there. He decided to let her know there were no hard feelings. Eventually. In the meantime, he would enjoy the Danish.

Kelli led her ten o'clock appointment to her now-empty office where she had menus, pricing, and samples all displayed. Kelli smiled while she gave the woman information and choices. Finally, after almost an hour, the woman made her decisions and wrote a check for a down payment. Kelli smiled and escorted her to the elevator.

Rushing back to the office, Kelli changed the samples, menus and pricing on display because another customer was coming on her lunchbreak at noon. While she waited, Kelli checked the website and social media pages for messages. There were two. She replied with information.

Her twelve o'clock appointment arrived, and Kelli decided she liked the woman, Susan Benning. They were about the same age, and Susan was single like Kelli. Her purpose was to plan a family gathering. She rented the second floor and decided on a menu for lunch but also added appetizers and sweets for an afternoon snack. After the decisions were made, Susan and Kelli sat and talked for a while. The two bonded over being single in a small town, and they got along so well they agreed to meet at the pizza restaurant for dinner.

Grant turned on the television. He watched a news program for exactly fifteen minutes. An hour later when he knew there was no headache or dizziness, he tried another fifteen minutes. The next time he tried twenty minutes. He kept increasing the amount of time in front of his TV screen until he reached an hour. No problems. He was glad. He would do the same procedure with his computer tomorrow.

At seven Grant was looking into his almost empty refrigerator, trying to decide if he needed to go to the cafe for dinner. He heard a knock on his door. He opened it, and a teenager stood there with a pizza and a card. He handed Grant the pizza and left.

Grant put the pizza on the island and opened the card. It was a 'thinking of you' card. The note at the bottom of the card said, *I really am sorry, Kelli.* Grant grinned. He knew she was sorry, but he enjoyed her apology. Sausage and mushrooms, his favorite. Now, how did she know that?

The next morning Grant had barely finished his cup of coffee when there was a knock at his door. He opened it to see Tracy there with a takeout breakfast and a card. Grant looked at Tracy as if trying to decipher what was going on. She just gave him an innocent look, turned, and went back down the stairs.

Back at the kitchen island, Grant saw that it was a full griddle breakfast. He opened the card. It was a welcome back to work card. The note at the bottom said. *Hope your first day back goes well. I am so sorry, Kelli.* He couldn't help it; he chuckled.

Grant had finished eating and cleaned up the kitchen when there was another knock at the door. He opened the door to see Paul walk into the apartment carrying Grant's laptop. Paul put the computer on the kitchen island.

"I got nosey and looked through your files," Paul admitted. "I knew the business had grown, but I had no idea of just how much. I looked through the connections, and they're perfect. I couldn't have done better myself. I probably would not have done that well. I'm particularly pleased with Bailey's analysis of a gap in transportation. I'm in the negotiating phase of forming a partnership with a local trucking company near there to expand to where we need help. If it works out, the Lohi Transport Company will get bigger and more profitable, and we will serve our vendors there."

Paul sat on a bar stool beside Grant. He looked Grant in the eye.

"Tell me what happened the other day," Paul said seriously.

Grant told him about getting annoyed with Kelli and going to the basement. He had never been there, and before he started to work, he looked around.

"I was admiring a vase in Candy's cabinet," Grant said. "It looked a lot like one my grandmother kept on her dining room table. I didn't hear the door open. Suddenly,

I heard Kelli scream then she hit me. I probably scared the daylights out of her. If I had known she was coming down, I would have turned around and spoken to her so I wouldn't startle her."

"Was her talking in her office with the door closed so loud that you felt you had to leave the floor?" Paul asked.

"It was loud. But if I had been patient, the call would have ended, and she would have left. I got annoyed and jumped the gun; I will admit that. So, yes, I think she could tone her conversations down a notch, but in all fairness, she had no idea I would be there. Why would she? I left my door closed. She couldn't see that I wasn't in the office."

"Did you know that she cleaned the basement, cried all day, and moved her entire office down there, minus the big furniture?" Paul asked.

"No. No one told me that," Grant replied. He felt a little sorry for Kelli.

Paul looked at Grant, "What about the candlestick you had Hank bag as evidence?"

"Get it back," Grant said with a sheepish grin. "Tell him he doesn't need it. I don't intend to press charges. I did that in the heat of the moment. I was in pain, and I was so mad at the woman I might have pressed charges if I hadn't been taken to the hospital. I'm not angry, now. My head no longer hurts, and I feel a little sorry for her. I know she hates what happened." Grant chuckled, "She has sent me I'm sorry food three times, now. She's definitely creative. Candy's lucky to have her."

"I'm glad you feel that way," Paul said, smiling with relief. "I was hoping we could all get past this and continue working together."

Grant said, "I would like that, too. I may work here for a few more days. I can only have screen time in increasing increments."

"Understandable," Paul said. "The funny part is that Bailey had no idea that anything was going on. She was in her own little world on the third floor. You should have seen her face when I told her what happened. I almost laughed."

Paul looked at his watch and stood, "I need to get going." He looked at Grant, "Baby steps."

"I understand," Grant said with a grin. "I don't want to mess up the healing process, either."

Grant tried working on the computer for fifteen minutes then waited. There were no problems, so he knew everything was going to be fine. He was impatient, but he followed the doctor's instructions.

At six Grant heard a knock at the door. Tracy was there holding another takeout plate. Grant chuckled and took it from her. Tracy grinned and went back down the steps. Grant opened it on the island. There was a steak, baked potato, salad and carrot cake.

He opened the card. It was a congratulations card. The note at the bottom said, *Welcome back to work. I am so sorry. Kelli.*

Grant burst into laughter. She was over the top. No one could stay angry with her, it was impossible.

*****

Grant went back to work full-time the following Wednesday. He had been out of the office for a week. Bailey was happy to see him and glad to share the on-call responsibility again. Grant gave her a day off with pay, her choice of day. She was happy about that.

The open door to Kelli's office made him stop. Just as Paul had said, all that was left was big furniture. Grant went to his office. The Ficus tree he had seen delivered to Kelli's office stood in front of a window. At first, he was confused, then he realized it needed sunlight. He tested the soil. It was dry. He got a coffee cup, filled it with water from the bathroom and watered the plant.

Kelli walked into the basement. The bright fluorescent lights and no windows made her remember the Ficus tree. She had meant to get it out of Grant's office before he arrived. Maybe she still had time. She ran up the stairs and opened the door to the third-floor hallway. Grant's office door was open. She stopped. He was bending over at the window and watering her plant.

Kellie watched Grant straighten up and turn toward her in the doorway. It was as if he sensed her presence.

"It needed water," Paul said in a gentle tone.

Kelli came into the room, "I'll get it out of your way."

"No," he said, "You can leave it. It needs the sunlight."

Grant looked at her. She had on a sundress that high-lighted her blue eyes. Her hair was in the standard pony-tail, so the straps and bodice of the dress were not obscured by hanging curls. There was a slight amount of cleavage above the V shaped neckline. He had not realized just how beautiful she was. She wouldn't look at him. Suddenly, Grant wanted to bridge the gap.

"Kelli," he said. Kelli looked at him. He saw misery in her eyes.

He grinned, "Thank you for all the I'm sorry food and

cards."

Tears welled in her eyes. "I really am sorry."

Grant walked toward her, "If I hadn't gotten annoyed and jumped the gun, I would not have been in the basement and would not have startled you."

"If I had taken the call downstairs, you would not have gotten annoyed," she replied.

Grant held out his hand, "Friends?"

Kelli smiled, walked forward, put her hand in his and said, "Friends."

Grant looked at her and asked, "Truce?"

Kelli smiled and said, "Truce."

Grant reached out and hugged Kelli. Kelli hugged him back. When they drew apart, each one was smiling. Grant thought Kelli looked like a weight had been lifted from her shoulders.

"The basement has got to be miserable," Grant said. "It's dark and probably claustrophobic. You can move back."

"Maybe not for a while," Kelli said. "The calls are getting more frequent and so are the appointments. We have events booked at least once a week through December."

"Your decision," Grant said, "But it will be okay when you do."

"Thank you." Kelli gestured to the door, "I guess I need to get back to work."

"And I need to start work," Grant said.

He watched Kelli leave then closed his door. He leaned back against it, closed his eyes and let out a long breath. That was easier than he thought it would be. What shocked him was the way she felt in his arms. He could get used to that, he thought, but that would really mess things up.

CHAPTER 11

Kelli continued to work in the basement, but she used the office on the third floor for appointments and displaying samples. She tried to be as quiet as possible and found if she toned down her own enthusiasm, the clients weren't as loud. Kelli considered that to be progress in her own professionalism.

The wall calendars that Kelli loved showed every Saturday night in August had an event booked. Kelli and the staff got to know each other and grew into an efficient team. Her days were full of phone calls, planning, organizing, and monitoring the website and social media. At night Kelli intended to use the motel's exercise room, but fell asleep not long after dinner. Some nights she fell asleep before taking off her makeup. She decided she needed to rearrange her days and schedules to make her health a priority.

One Monday, several weeks into her job, Kelli had a rare day with no appointments. She decided to take the day off. She drove to the park on Main Street and ran for exercise. Kelli emptied her mind of work issues and concentrated on the sound of her feet hitting the ground as she ran.

Halfway through the trail, Kelli was running through a pleasant area of shade. She looked up in surprised and grinned when she ran into Grant going the opposite way on the trail. He smiled, turned around and started running with her. They ran in companionable silence until they had completed the circuit and were back at the parking lot.

"I didn't know you ran here in the mornings," Kelli said panting. She began stretching out her muscles.

"Well, I didn't know you did, either," Grant answered as he wiped sweat from his forehead with the hem of his shirt.

"I just started," Kelli said. She drank from her water bottle. "I've gotten so busy I found I was leaving exercise out of my day. I need to find a way to reinsert it. Sometimes I'm just so tired I can't use the exercise room at night."

Grant nodded knowingly as he drank his own water. The two sat on a bench near the front of the park.

"I understand," he said. "After all my inactivity from the head injury, I found myself getting winded climbing the stairs to the office."

He saw Kelli wince.

"I'm so sorry," she said again. "I don't think I will ever say that enough to you."

"Kelli," he said. "It's over and forgotten. Are you going to the office from here?"

"No," she told him. "I'm taking a day off. I have worked every Saturday for almost six weeks. I need to seriously look at a way to streamline my days so that I can have a five-day work week."

"Yes, you do," he said. "Either Bailey or I have to be on call every week night until eight o'clock to answer questions from the west coast. I schedule us so that we still only work forty hours a week. Maybe you should talk with Candy about an assistant. I know you've grown her business."

"Maybe after the end of the year when we see the profits," Kelli said. "In the meantime, I'm going to try and find time for more exercise. That will help."

Grant stood and stretched.

"Let me know your schedule," he said. "If it works out, maybe we could run together. It helps to have a running buddy to keep me focused and accountable. Otherwise, it's too easy to skip it."

Kelli stood and smiled. "I know what you mean. I'll work on that today and let you know tomorrow. Thanks for the run." Kelli opened the door to her car. "I have some serious shopping to do for transition clothes for the fall

"Good luck with that," he said and watched Kelli back out of her parking slot and drive away from the park. The idea of fall and winter clothes made him a little sad. He liked those sundresses with the little straps.

CHAPTER 12

The weekend of the Hicks/Blalock wedding arrived. The rehearsal dinner with its baseball theme was a success, and the red and blue decorations had been removed. Now, the second floor had been transformed into a reception venue with flowers and decorations in white and various shades of pink. The staff was waiting for the wedding party and guests to arrive. Kelli walked through the room one more time, straightening chairs and centerpieces. Everything was in place.

"Relax, it's perfect," Candy said, patting Kelli on the shoulder and watching the staff placing food over the hot water. "When we get the other building open, we can enlarge this space. I'm having Chip increase the size of the staging area, so we can have everything up here at the same time. Then we won't have to make so many trips up and down the elevator after the guests arrive. That's difficult when we and the guests are trying to use the same one. Maybe someday we can afford a service elevator."

"That sounds good," Kelli replied as she pushed a rolling cart farther behind a partition so it couldn't be seen by the guests in the dining area. "How long will the construction take?"

"The engineers said four weeks at the most for them to open the wall and brace it for support," Candy said. "Then another six weeks or more for Chip and Jacob to work their magic. They will start with the second floor first so we can have the venue open for Halloween."

Their conversation was cut short when the first of the guests started to arrive. The staff directed everyone to appetizers and the beverage table. Finally, the DJ announced the bridal party. The bride and groom arrived to the applause and cheers of the wedding guests, and Kelli had the staff uncover the buffet. The meal flowed smoothly, the bride and groom cut the cake, and the DJ began his entertainment.

Kelli was helping the staff remove the buffet pans from the table when she heard her name. She turned around to see Grant.

"Grant! This is the second event you have been to. Are you a crasher?" she said with a grin.

"No," he said smiling. "The groom is a cousin. His mother is my father's older sister."

"Nice family," Kelli said smiling. "I've enjoyed working with both sides of the I do's."

Kelli heard Grant's name called through the crowd, so she turned to finish the task of breaking down the buffet set.

"Grant!" the man called.

Kelli looked up to see a man approaching who was slightly shorter but heavier than Grant. The paunch at his abdomen made the spaces between his shirt's buttons gape. He had brown hair and brown eyes. Kelli gave a shiver. Everything about him seemed too slick, too arrogant for her.

"Good to see you," the man said to Grant. "Are you going to introduce me to the beautiful woman you were just talking with?"

Grant rolled his eyes and sighed.

"Kelli," he said, looking apologetic, "this is the groom's brother, Aaron Blalock. Aaron, this is Kelli Mills. She manages the events and catering company that did the rehearsal dinner and the reception."

Kelli was grateful that she had hands full of pans and serving utensils.

"Nice to meet you, Aaron," Kelli replied politely. "Now if you two will excuse me, I'm on the job."

"Not so fast, Kelli," Aaron said arrogantly. He raised his eyebrows as his eyes traveled across her body. "I want to get to know you."

"Sorry," Kelli replied quickly, feeling repulsed. "No time. As I said, I'm working. There are a few bridesmaids looking your way. I think they want to dance."

Aaron turned around to see who she was talking about, and Kelli took the chance to sneak past Grant and behind the divider to the staging area in the back of the room. When Aaron turned back around, she was gone.

"Where did she go?" he asked Grant.

"Wherever the staff goes when they're working," he said to Aaron and trying not to smile.

Kelli stood behind the divider and placed the dishes on a rolling cart. She was close enough to hear the conversation between Grant and Aaron, so she waited, intentionally eavesdropping.

"Don't you work in the building? Where is she?" Aaron

asked, looking around the room.

"I work on the top floor," Grant said, drawing Aaron's attention away from the staging divider. "I have nothing to do with the first two floors, the bakery or the catering business. Besides, she's working, Aaron. Don't get her in trouble." Grant had never really liked Aaron, and he was getting frustrated with Aaron's persistence in talking with Kelli.

Aaron looked at him and a sudden look of understanding came into his eyes.

"Oh, I get it," Aaron said. "You're interested in her, and you're warning me off. Too bad, big guy, unless you're married, she's fair game."

Grant's irritation and frustration with his cousin was growing.

"Come back to the reception, Aaron," Grant said, taking Aaron by the arm and leading him to the bridal party. "Dance with one of the bridesmaids and have some cake. The woman is working. She doesn't have time to talk with either of us."

When Kelli realized that Aaron had left the buffet area, she came back into the room to finish retrieving the rest of the setup.

She caught Grant's eye and mouthed, "Thank you." Grant smiled and nodded in understanding.

The sun had set, and the party was winding down. The newlyweds left the venue, and guests began leaving. Aaron took the elevator to the main floor and left the building. His car was parked in front of the café.

Aaron drummed his fingers on the steering wheel. He was annoyed with his cousin. Grant probably thought of himself as a big man, a knight in shining armor protecting Kelli from him. He was the man interested in getting to know her, not Grant.

Taking a flask from his pocket, Aaron took a large gulp of whiskey. He thought it was just too bad for Grant, because he was going to lose Kelli. Aaron confidently thought of himself as the better man to woo the beautiful woman. Aaron smiled, thinking about how nice it would be when Kelli was his girlfriend. There was no way she could resist him.

Aaron was still sitting in his car on Main Street, watching the second floor of the bakery building. He could see the catering staff clearing the reception area. The flask of whiskey was almost empty when Aaron noticed Grant standing on the venue's balcony, watching him. Aaron grinned at Grant and started his car. After giving Grant a middle finger, he drove around the block to the back of the building. All he had to do was wait until Kelli finished her job and left, then he could take her to dinner.

Grant stood on the balcony while the staff finished sweeping the floor.

"Hey," Kelli said as she came up to him. "We're getting ready to close and lock the doors. You've been hanging around for a while. Is there a problem?"

Grant pointed to a car that was backing out of a parking place on Main Street.

"That's Aaron's car," he said. "I think he's waiting for you to get off. If you're interested in him, I will back off. But if you're not interested, I can run interference and keep him away."

"Eww no, please keep him away," Kelli exclaimed, turning up her nose. "How can you be related to that guy? You're nothing alike. I mean, you may get short tempered and testy with me, but you're a nice guy. Your cousin is a creep. He sizes women up with his eyes very disrespectfully. All my staff noticed that about him. Plus, he's arrogant. He thinks he's nature's gift to women."

Grant laughed out loud. "I've never heard him called that, but if that's how you feel, then I'll let him know you're not interested."

The staff was gone. Kelli turned out the lights, and Grant rode the elevator down to the first floor with her. Kelli walked to the front door of the building.

"Do you want me to let you out the front door before I lock it?" she asked.

Grant shook his head. "No, it's dark. I'll walk you to your car like a gentleman. Gotta make my mama proud," he said with a grin and a wink.

Grant watched while Kelli turned off the bakery kitchen's lights and locked its interior back door. Then he followed her to the back door of the building where she locked it behind them. As they started walking to her car, Kelli heard her name. She turned to see Aaron standing in the parking area. She was suddenly grateful for the streetlights illuminating the area and for Grant's presence.

"Kelli, I waited to see if you wanted to go somewhere for a drink," Aaron said.

"No, thank you, Aaron," Kelli said. "It's been a long day, and I'm tired. I just want to go home and get some rest."

"I'll be glad to take you home," he said as he took a few steps toward Kelli.

Kelli was starting to get apprehensive. She took a couple steps backward, away from Aaron, and felt her back hit the brick wall of the building. Feeling trapped, her heart rate increased and her chest tightened.

Grant stepped in front of Kelli.

"Back off Aaron," Grant said, his back to Kelli. "She doesn't want to go with you."

"And I suppose she wants to go with you?" Aaron asked.

"Yes, Aaron," Kelli said before Grant could answer. Kelli took Grant's arm. "That's exactly what's going to happen. I'm going with Grant." She slipped Grant her car keys and said, "He's going to take me home."

Grant walked over to Kelli's car and unlocked it. He opened the passenger door for her and helped her in.

"Why do I not believe you?" Aaron asked, his voice slurred slightly from the whiskey.

"Think what you want," Grant said. "The truth is she doesn't want to go with you. She wants to go with me."

"I find that hard to believe," Aaron said, crossing his arms. "Who would choose you over me?"

"Evidently, Kelli did," Grant said. "Now, if you will step out of the way, we will leave."

Aaron hesitated, then moved away from Kelli's car. He got into his own car and watched as Grant turned the key in the ignition.

"Where to?" Grant asked Kelli as they heard the engine start.

"You can't take me home," Kelli said. "You don't have a car to get back. Just go around to the back of your place. I'll drop you off and then drive home."

"Okay," Grant said. He looked back to see Aaron driving across the parking lot. Grant was annoyed that Aaron followed them closely and had his headlights on bright.

Grant pulled out of the parking area and onto the side street.

When he started toward the main street, he said, "Great. The jerk is following us. I'm taking you to my place. I don't want him to know where you live."

Kelli turned around to see Aaron's overly bright headlights following them.

"Alright. Let's do that," Kelli said. "You're right, I don't want him to know where I live. Is he always this creepy?"

"I have no idea," Grant said. "I haven't had any contact with him in several years. I don't know what he's like. He's several years older than I am, so we never really had a lot to do with each other as kids.

Grant drove down Main Street. Aaron followed him. Grant turned onto a side street. Aaron followed him. Grant turned onto the back street behind the café. Aaron followed him.

When he parked Kelli's car beside his own in the lot behind the café, Grant handed Kelli a key.

"This is the key to the back door of the building. Get out, unlock the door and go inside. Watch from there. I will confront Aaron."

"He won't hurt you, will he?" she asked.

"No. Besides, I'm bigger than he is," Grant said giving her a grin. "But have your cellphone out. If we get surprised, you can call 911."

Kelli got out of the car, ran to the door and unlocked it. She stepped inside and took out her cellphone. Then she opened the door slightly to watch what was happening outside.

Aaron rolled down his driver's window when Grant

approached his car.

"What are you doing, Aaron?" Grant asked. "Leave Kelli alone. She's tired and wants nothing more than to get a good night's sleep."

Aaron was drunk. Grant saw an empty whiskey bottle on the passenger's seat. Fast food wrappers and empty beer cans littered the floor on the passenger's side.

Aaron slurred, "She would have gone with me if you hadn't interfered. You'll be sorry when she realizes what she missed out on and is mad at you."

Grant was glad it was dark and that Aaron couldn't see the look of disgust that crossed his face.

"Go home, Aaron. Sleep off your drunk. Kelli doesn't plan on going anywhere tonight." Grant turned and walked to the back door of the building.

Kelli heard Grant talking with Aaron. She watched Grant shake his head and start walking toward her. He entered the building, then closed and locked the door behind them.

"What's he going to do?" she asked.

"I don't know," Grant said. "He's drunk. He must have brought his own liquor, because you didn't serve any at the reception. Let's go upstairs. We can look out the back window and make sure he leaves."

Grant led Kelli up the interior stairwell and unlocked the door to the apartment. He held the door for Kelli and turned on the lights in the living area.

"The only window to the parking area is in my room." he told her.

Grant led Kelli to his bedroom. He left the lights off and closed the door so the lights from the rest of the apartment would not show through the window and give them away. They looked down at the ground. Aaron had parked behind both Grant and Kelli's cars. There was no way she could get out and go home until he moved.

"Looks like we're stuck unless you want to call the police. As soon as you get in your car, he's going to follow you," Grant said.

"No. Don't call the police," Kelli said, "at least not yet. I don't want any negative publicity for the venue or catering company. All we need is for people to hear that a stalker was outside the bakery building. Then no one would ever want to book the place or go into the bakery or schedule a catered event. Then I would be out of a job, and I like it here. I like this job."

Grant closed the blinds and turned the bedroom light on.

"Wow," Kelli said. "This is nice." She looked inside the large bathroom. "What does the rest of the place look like?"

Grant gave her a tour. As they walked through the apartment, Kelli noticed the neutral walls and floors, comfortable furniture, and the colorful accents of pillows, art, rugs, and linens.

"If you ever decide to move, let me know," Kelli said, "I would like to live here."

"It came furnished," Grant said. "Paul lived here. When they built their new house, he left this furniture and let Candy furnish the new place like she wanted."

"Sweet," Kelli said. "I especially like the commute; you just walk across the street. I'm renting an extended stay apartment at the motel at the interstate. There were no other furnished apartments around here when I was looking for one."

"I have all my stuff in storage if you need to borrow something," he said. "Unless you like living there."

"Definitely not," she said. "But I have a six month's lease, so I'm stuck until December."

Kelli sighed and dropped heavily onto the couch.

"Drat!" she exclaimed, closing her eyes. "All I wanted to do was shower and go to bed."

Grant went back into his bedroom. He returned and handed her a T-shirt and a pair of gym shorts. Walking back down the hall, he turned on the lights in the hall bathroom and extra bedroom.

"Shower here," he said pointing to the bathroom, "and you can sleep in the spare bedroom. Surely, he'll be gone by morning. Tomorrow is Sunday so you won't have to rush back to change and get to work."

Kelli hesitated a moment then said, "Thanks. I appreciate this."

"There are towels in the cabinet, and there should be shampoo and body wash in the shower. Help yourself. I'll turn off the lights out here and I'll see you in the morning. First one up makes coffee," he said, grinning.

Kelli chuckled. "You got it."

Kelli went into the bathroom. Grant locked the apartment door, turning the interior deadbold that he rarely used. Then he turned out the lights, and went to his bedroom. Never in a million years would he have thought he would have to come to Kelli's rescue. Shaking his head at the unusual events of the night, Grant got ready for bed.

CHAPTER 13

The next morning, Kelli woke up. She sleepily opened her eyes and immediately closed them. That was not her ceiling and this was not her bed. This was not her apartment. Then she remembered that she was in Grant's apartment.

Becoming more awake, Kelli remembered the reception. Memories of Aaron at the reception then trying to take her to dinner flashed through her mind, making her shudder. Memories of Grant coming to her rescue and bringing her to his apartment made her smile. Grant made her feel safe.

Kelli yawned, got out of bed, and slowly walked to the bathroom. She shuddered as she saw herself in the mirror. She had gone to bed with wet hair, and she had the worst bed head. Her hair looked like a poodle that had not been groomed in six months. Running her fingers through her hair, she pulled it back with the ponytail holder. She got dressed, wishing she had a toothbrush.

Kelli went into the hallway and found Grant sitting at the kitchen island drinking coffee and watching a news program on TV. She walked over to the cabinet and poured herself a cup of coffee.

"There's cream and sugar on the counter," Grant told her, pointing to the area to the right of the coffee maker.

Kelli shook her head no.

"Black. Black and strong," she mumbled.

Grant chuckled. No matter how hard she had tried, her hair would not be tamed.

After Kelli had a few sips he asked, "Feeling human?"

"Ummm," she said nodding. "I'm not coherent until I have coffee." She looked at him over the rim of her cup, "You look nice. I, on the other hand, look like something the cat dragged in, or a real sleezy walk of shame."

Grant laughed.

"You're fine," he said. "I'll find you a hairbrush and a toothbrush. Then I'm sure you'll feel better." He walked back to his bedroom and returned with the promised toiletries.

"Thank you," she said. Kelli put her coffee on the counter and said, "Keep my coffee warm. This may take a while."

Grant chuckled and said, "I'm going to look out the window and see if Aaron is still there," and he walked down the hall to his bedroom. Looking out the window, he saw that Aaron's car was still behind the building, blocking both of their cars. Evidently, Aaron hadn't moved all night. He sighed. He was going to have to go down and confront him.

He walked back into the kitchen and sat down to finish his coffee. Ten minutes later, Kelli walked confidently out of the bathroom, her hair brushed and in its professional ponytail.

"Is he gone?" she asked.

"Believe it or not, he's still there. I'm going to have to go down and wake him up. He's bound to be hungover." Grant started to go out the door but hesitated and looked back at Kelli. "Get your cell phone and watch from the back windows. If there's a real problem I will look up and yell call 911."

"OK." Kelli went into the guest bedroom, got her cell phone then walked back to Grant's room and stood by the window. She could see Aaron's car still parked behind the cafe, blocking her car. A few minutes later she saw Grant going out the back door.

Grant knocked on Aaron's window. Aaron was sleeping so soundly that Grant could hear his snoring. Grant knocked again. He sighed and pulled the handle on the driver's door. It wasn't locked.

Once the door was opened, Grant shook Aaron's shoulder.

"Wake up. Aaron, wake up!" Grant said loudly.

Aaron opened his eyes and looked up at Grant. "What? Grant?"

"You were drunk. You slept in this parking lot all night. Go home, Aaron," Grant ordered.

Aaron seemed to be more awake. He looked around. "Did you stay here last night with Kelli?" he asked angrily.

"Yes, Aaron, I did," Grant answered tersely. He felt his frustration with Aaron growing. "You parked behind our cars and blocked us in."

Aaron scowled and looked at Grant. Staring back at Aaron, Grant saw a myriad of emotions cross Aaron's face. Aaron looked angry, then frustrated, then he squinted at Grant. Aaron stared at Grant for almost a full minute.

"Well," sneered Aaron. "We'll see about this." Giving Grant an arrogant smile, Aaron started his car.

Grant backed away from Aaron and watched as his cousin drove out of the parking area. He wondered what Aaron had meant with that last comment but sighed in relief that the man was gone. He turned and went back into the building.

Kelli had been watching from the bedroom window. She watched Grant knock on the window of the car then open the driver's door and shake Aaron awake. Grant talked to the man for a few minutes. Eventually, Aaron started his car and drove away. Grant came back up the stairs.

Kelli met him in the kitchen. "That looked interesting," she said.

"He was asleep. It took a minute to get him awake, but I did. He looked like he had one heck of a headache. I told him to go home, which is what I hope he's doing. I'm not sure where he lives. Greensboro, maybe? We lost touch years ago. He was older, left home, and rarely came to any family gatherings. Plus, I didn't care enough about him to reach out and maintain any semblence of a relationship."

"I can understand why," Kelli said. "You're nothing alike. It's hard to keep a relationship going where you have nothing in common. I have family members that I've lost touch with, too."

Kelli picked up her cup and said, "More coffee please. Pleeaassee."

Grant chuckled and refilled her cup from the still hot coffee pot.

"What do you want me to do with your clothes?" Kelli asked as she finished her coffee.

"Just leave them on the bed," he answered. "I'll put them in the wash the next time I do a load."

"I guess I'd better be going," she said. Kelli walked over to Grant and placed a hand on his arm. "I really do appreciate what you did for me last night. The guy may be your cousin, but he was beginning to scare me. I don't think I ever want to see him again, anywhere."

Grant looked at the hand on his arm then into Kelli's eyes.

"Aaron should be afraid of you," he said. "You have a nasty swing with a candlestick in your hand."

Kelli looked shocked until she realized Grant was teasing. Then she made a face at him.

"I was glad to help," he said, "and I agree with your opinion about Aaron. I always thought he had a cruel streak and was a bully, so I would steer clear of him."

Grant thought he was about to drown in Kelli's blue eyes. A new type of tension had started between them. He wanted to pull her closer and kiss her, but he didn't. They were beginning to have a congenial relationship, and he didn't want to make it awkward. Instead, he smiled and walked her to her car.

Kelli drove her SUV to the edge of the parking area, looking around to make sure Aaron had really gone. She couldn't believe how nervous she was from the whole encounter. She turned onto the side street then onto Main Street. With each turn, she expected to see Aaron's car, and she was relieved when it wasn't there.

Driving back to her motel, Kelli also felt disappointment. She had wanted Grant to kiss her, but she had been afraid to kiss him first. If he had rejected her, she would have been embarrassed and things at work would have been even more awkward than they already were. But if he had made the first move and she had not responded well, things would have been just as awkward. Kelli sighed. She would have to settle for friendship. At least now they were getting along and wouldn't be yelling at each other.

CHAPTER 14

Monday morning Kelli dressed carefully. It was early September, but it was still hot. She pulled on a royal blue jacket over a matching sundress that sported tiny straps, a low cut back, and V shaped neckline. Slipping on a pair of sandals with heels, she drove to work.

Kelli stopped in at the bakery and got three coffees to take upstairs. When she got off the elevator, she handed the first one to Bailey. Bailey thanked her with a smile.

Going into her office, Kelli put her purse, bag, and coffee on her desk. She took her jacket off and draped it over her chair. Picking up the last coffee she tapped on Grant's door.

"Come in," echoed through the door.

Kelli opened the door, put the coffee on the desk and turned around to leave. Grant saw the cup, looked up and saw Kelli's retreating form.

"Thank you," he said.

"You're welcome," she said as she turned to look at him.

Kelli felt a slight flush as she looked at Grant, sitting there, all handsome with his dark hair and green eyes.

She sighed and turned back to the door.

Grant could not believe his eyes. She wore her hair down. Strawberry blond curls caressed her shoulders and hid the tiny straps on her dress. The dress was cut low across her back and had a low v shaped neckline in the front. She had never worn anything like that to work before. The thought crossed his mind that she might have done it for his benefit. He realized that he hoped that was the case because she definitely had his attention.

Their eyes locked for a moment, but the spell between them was broken when Kelli's phone rang. She hurried back to her office where she had temporarily put her belongings.

Kelli closed the door behind her and said, "Cotton Catering and Events," in a low voice into her phone.

Grant thought that either she was speaking in a lower tone, or he was having an easier time tuning her out, because he was able to get back to work quickly. The phone rang several more times. She had been right; Mondays were the busiest phone days. Thank goodness she was speaking in a softer voice.

Grant heard the phone ring again and Kelli answered it. He heard a tapping on his door. Kelli stood there with the phone in her hand. She pushed the button placing the phone on speaker then put a finger to her lips asking him to listen and not speak. Grant immediately recognized the voice on the phone. It was Aaron Blalock telling her how great Saturday night had been.

He could see that Kelli was nervous, because her hand trembled as she placed the phone between them on his desk. Kelli masked it well, because her voice was calm when she spoke.

"I'm glad you enjoyed the meal Saturday night," she said. "Cotton Catering and Events was happy to serve your family."

"Now, Kelli," Aaron said in a condescending tone, "Let's be honest. Our enjoyment was more than a meal. We enjoyed meeting each other, admit it." Kelli's eyes got wide, and she made a gagging gesture. It took all of Grant's willpower to not laugh out loud.

"I don't know what you mean, Aaron," she answered. "I was on the job. It's my place to be nice to everyone."

"I could take nice to another level," Aaron said suggestively. "Have dinner with me."

"No thank you, Aaron. I'm afraid I can't do that," Kelli answered, her brow furrowed with stress. She was glad that she was sitting down in the chair in front of Grant's desk.

Grant watched Kelli as she spoke. He could see the stress in her expression.

"Sure, you can," Aaron said. "I will pick you up at the bakery at six. We can go to a nice restaurant in Winston, and I will have you home by nine."

"No thank you, Aaron," she repeated. "I still can't do that."

"Why?" Aaron asked, an arrogance in his voice. "I know you don't have a boyfriend. No self-respecting man would let his woman work on a Saturday night."

"Aaron, I'm going to be blunt," Kelli said. "I don't want to go out with you."

Aaron's laughter echoed through the phone.

"You're a funny girl, Kelli. I like that," he said. "We'll have a lot of fun together."

"Aaron, listen to me, I will not go out with you," Kelli

said firmly.

"Yes, you will," he answered, calmly and firmly. Kelli thought she heard the hint of a threat in his voice.

Grant held up his hand to Kelli, indicating he wanted to talk, and leaned over the desk to the phone.

"Aaron, this is Grant."

"Grant! What are you doing in my girl's office?" Aaron asked.

Kelli threw up her hands in frustration. Grant looked annoyed, but he locked eyes with Kelli again, trying to convey understanding.

"First of all," Grant said, "she is not your girl. Second, she has told you she is not going out with you. Third, to press the issue with her is harassment and stalking, which is against the law. Be careful, Aaron. Her boss has a lawyer as a family friend."

"She wouldn't sick the law on me," Aaron said confidently. "We're meant to be together, and she knows it."

Grant had a determined look on his face.

"Aaron, she is not your girl," Grant said firmly.

"Yeah? How can you be so sure unless she's your girl. Wait, are y'all a couple?" Aaron asked.

Grant looked Kelli in the eye and said, "Yes. As a matter of fact, we are. We have been seeing each other since almost the first day she started to work here. So, I would appreciate it if you would not harass my girlfriend."

Kelli gave him a look of astonishment. Grant looked sheepish and shrugged.

"Girlfriend, huh," Aaron said. "Why do I feel like you're lying? If she's your girlfriend, bring her to Mom and Dad's this coming Sunday. They're having a little gathering to welcome the newlyweds back home. If she's your girlfriend, she will be glad to come and meet the family. If she refuses, well, I will consider her fair game, and bro, the game will be on. Then I will be the winner of that gorgeous face and body."

Kelli's stomach churned. Who was this man, and how could anyone be so delusional about his own appeal to women?

Frustrated and angry, Grant ended the call abruptly.

"I'm sorry, Kelli," he said. His eyes had not left hers. "But I didn't know what else to do. Being in a relationship is the only way he will leave you alone. We're going to have to go to a small family reunion, otherwise he will be camping on your doorstep, refusing to take no for an answer."

Kelli wrapped her arms around her stomach. Suddenly she felt cold and scared. Calm, patient, and practical with good common sense had always been the hallmark of her personality. Now she was scared and bordering on panic. Turning, Kelli walked back to her office and put her jacket on, trying to get warm.

Grant followed Kelli into her office. He saw her put the jacket on. She sat in one of the chairs in front of her desk trying to catch her breath. She was deliberately slowing her breathing. She was scared and his family was to blame.

Taking Kelli's hand, Grant led her back to his office where a couch sat against their common wall. He made her sit and then sat beside her. He put his arm around her and rubbed her back and arms.

"Slow your breathing," he said. "You're having a mild panic attack, which is understandable."

Kelli nodded, indicating that she knew what was happening. Grant went to a small refrigerator behind his desk and got a bottle of water.

"Here," he said, handing her the bottle. "Drink this and slow your breathing." Kelli took the bottle of water. Her hand was trembling, but he could see she was beginning to regain control.

"Thank you," she said, taking a drink of water. "I just suddenly panicked. I've never done that before."

"I imagine you've never had a stalker before," he replied.

"True," Kelly said. She looked at her watch. "I have an appointment with a potential client in fifteen minutes, I need to get ready." She looked at Grant, "Thank you."

When she stood to go back to her office, Grant pulled her into a hug and said, "It's going to be fine. Just a party on Sunday, and it will be all over." Kelli hugged him back.

Grant watched Kelli as she walked back to her office. With her jacket on, she looked crisp and professional. He knew she was worried, and maybe a little scared, but it was impressive to watch her put on a professional demeanor as she prepared for her client.

CHAPTER 15

On Sunday afternoon, Grant picked Kelli up at her apartment. He drove south on the interstate but turned off at the first exit. He followed Highway 268 for about five miles before turning off the bypass into Troy. Grant's aunt and uncle lived in an older part of the town in a large, historic home. Kelli was enchanted by the neighborhood as they neared the house.

"These homes are amazing," she said. "Imagine growing up in a house like this."

"They bought theirs just a few years ago," he said. "Their children were already grown, and some had left the nest. The groom last week was their baby. He has three older siblings. My parents will be here, too. They were at the wedding, but you were working, and I had no idea it would have been prudent to introduce you."

Kelli looked alarmed. "Do they know I'm the one who gave you a skull fracture?"

Grant laughed, "No. I told them all along it was an accident."

Kelli looked at him, "You did? Even when you were mad

at me?"

Grant smiled and said, "Yes. Even when I was mad at you. I mean, what man wants to admit that he got his skull cracked by a helpless female."

"What?" she exclaimed. "Helpless female? I don't think so. If you don't believe me, just ask the guy that I sent to the hospital with a skull fracture because I thought he was a burglar!"

"Okay," Grant said, laughing. "Not a helpless female."

Kelli grinned. She liked the bantering Grant over the testy Grant. Kelli turned from the window to watch Grant as he drove.

"How fascinated are people going to be that you brought a woman home to a family event?" she asked.

"Uh," he groaned. "They will be shocked. I've never had a serious girlfriend; expect the attention. Just be honest. We met on the job, became friends, and now we're seeing if there is more than friendship."

"Sounds good," Kelli said.

Grant parked at the sidewalk in front of the house. He got out, walked around and opened the passenger door for Kelli. She got out looking fresh in a pale yellow dress with neutral espadrille sandals. The dress was sleeveless with a square neckline just below her clavicle. It was totally unlike the sundress she had worn to work but very appropriate for meeting someone's family. Kelli took Grant's arm, and he led her around the house to the back patio where a crowd of people had gathered. Kelli was surprised at how many of the men looked similar to Grant.

As they rounded the corner of the house, Kelli held Grant's arm tighter when everyone stopped talking and stared at them.

"Smile," Grant whispered as he patted Kelli's hand. "Everyone is looking at you." He bent to her ear and quietly said, "Pretend you're madly in love with me. I dare you."

"You're on," Kelli said with a chuckle, "but you have to pretend, too."

Grant winked and said, "I can act better than you can."

"We'll see about that," Kelli answered playfully.

Grant led Kelli to two people and introduced them to her as his parents. Then he introduced her to his aunt and uncle. After that, his relatives took turns to meet the woman Grant had finally brought home to the family.

Whether they were standing or sitting, Kelli touched Grant's fingers or his arm. Grant responded by holding her hand at times. At one point she sat with his mother, and he left to go talk with his father. Kelli followed him with her eyes then had to force herself to concentrate on what his mother was saying.

It was beginning to grow dark when Grant said, "Come with me." He led her by the hand to the back of the yard. He pointed to a tall plant and said, "Watch."

Just at the point of darkness, yellow flowers began to open all over the plant. Kelli watched one after the other open to the evening's waning light.

"I've never seen anything like this," Kelli whispered. "I mean, you see time lapse pictures, but this is real, right in front of me. It's beautiful."

Grant smiled. "I thought you might like to see this. It's called evening primrose. It's one of my favorite plants. Mom has several.

Kelli watched the flowers in fascination. Grant

watched Kelli then put his index finger on her chin and turned her face to his. He bent down and kissed her. Kelli put her arms around him and kissed him back. The kiss was everything she thought it could be. It was caring and gentle yet gave the promise of passion being held in check.

Grant knew the minute his lips met Kelli's that he was lost. He had never felt like this for a woman in his entire life. He cherished every moment of that kiss and wanted more.

The two came back to reality when they heard a slow clap.

"Well, well, well." Aaron stood watching them and clapping. "You two know how to put on a good show."

"What are you doing?" growled Grant. "Have you resorted to spying?"

Aaron looked at Kelli, "What are you doing with this loser when you could have a real man?"

"You're awful, you know that?" Kelli said, her voice laden with disgust. "You can't believe a woman might not be interested in you, so you resort to stalking and derision. You're pathetic."

Aaron grew angry.

"Watch how you talk to me," Aaron said in a menacing tone. "I won't stand for my woman giving me any lip."

"I am not your woman!" exclaimed Kelli. "Get that through your thick skull, you neanderthal."

Kelli, Grant, and Aaron turned to see people approaching them along the path that meandered through the backyard.

"What's going on here?" asked Grant's uncle.

Kelli looked at him and said, "I'm sorry for disrupting

your party, but I'm asking you to keep your son, Aaron, away from me. If he continues to stalk me, I will have him arrested. I don't care if you are related to Grant. I will protect myself."

Aaron's father looked at Grant. "Is this true? Aaron has been stalking your young lady?"

"I'm sorry, Uncle," Grant said. "He tried to follow her home from the reception. He harassed her with a phone call, and will not take no for an answer. I told him, and Kelli told him that she and I are seeing each other and that she does not want anything to do with him. He doesn't seem to want to listen."

Grant turned to Kelli, "I think we should go now."

Kelli nodded in agreement. They started back toward the house. They stopped to say goodbye to Grant's parents then walked around the house to where they were parked.

"Do you think Aaron believed this?" Kelli asked.

"I don't see how he couldn't. I had a hard time remembering it wasn't true," Grant said.

"I know. Me too," Kelli said, nodding. She thought about the evening and decided she would like very much to be Grant's girlfriend and see where a relationship with him could go, but she would never admit it. Not when they had to work in the same office.

CHAPTER 16

Two days had passed since Grant's family gathering, and Aaron had not contacted Kelli. Grant was starting to believe that his ruse with Kelli had worked or that Aaron's family had pressured him to leave her alone. He got ready for work and walked into the café to get an egg biscuit and coffee to go.

"Just a minute, Mr. Sparks." Grant turned to see Tracy walking toward him, carrying a tray of rolled silverware.

"Yes?" he asked.

"I got a call from my mother last night. It seems word has spread all over Troy that the elusive Grant Sparks has a girlfriend and that her name is Kelli Mills. Care to explain?" she asked.

Grant sighed and looked around the packed dining room.

"Can we go to your office?" he asked. He didn't want this conversation to be heard by anyone nearby.

Tracy turned and led him back to her office and closed the door behind him.

"Alright," she said. "What's going on? Just three weeks ago, you couldn't stand the woman. Now the word is you two are an item."

"I can explain," Grant replied. "The wedding reception a week ago was for my cousin. I was there. Aaron Blalock, the groom's brother, was there too. He had been drinking." Grant raised his hands when Tracy started to protest.

"I know," Grant said, "Cotton Catering did not serve alcohol. He brought his own. I was talking with Kelli, complimenting her on the reception and the food when Aaron came up and demanded to be introduced. Kelli didn't want to talk to him and pointed him toward some women who wanted to dance. She took the chance to escape and hid behind the partition in the back until Aaron started dancing with a bridesmaid.

"Everyone was leaving, and the staff was cleaning up. I walked out onto the balcony and looked down at the street. Aaron was sitting in his car. Just sitting there, watching the building and waiting. I was afraid he would try to intercept Kelli when she went to her car. So, I warned her and helped her lock up the building.

"When we went out the back, he was waiting for her. Kelli slipped me her car keys and told Aaron she was leaving with me. I was going to take her home, but the idiot followed me. We decided to go back to my place until he left, then she could take her car and go home. But he never left. He parked behind our cars, blocking us in and went to sleep.

"That left Kelli trapped. So, she slept in the guest bedroom. The next morning, I woke Aaron up and told him to go home. I thought that was the end of it, but on Monday morning he called Kelli on her company phone. She came into my office and put it on speaker. Tracy, he's delusional. He thinks he and Kelli are a couple."

Tracy looked at him in shock and disbelief.

Grant continued, "I finally told him that Kelli was not interested in him because she was my girlfriend. He called my bluff. I had to take Kelli to a family gathering Sunday evening in Troy. I introduced her to everyone there as my girlfriend. We even played the part by holding hands, smiling and watching each other. I took her to the back of the yard to show her the evening primroses. Aaron followed and confronted us, accusing us of lying. His parents and the whole party heard him shouting and came back to see what was going on. Kelli was kind but firm when she told his parents that if Aaron didn't leave her alone, she would press charges against him for harassment and stalking."

"Oh, my word," Tracy said. "I had no idea that was going on. How is Kelli?"

"Nervous," Grant answered. "She's constantly looking all around when she needs to leave the building, and she jumps when the phone rings instead of quickly reaching for it expecting business. Two days have gone by without hearing from Aaron. I just hope that continues and he's out of her life.

"Poor girl. Do Candy and Paul know about this?" Tracy asked.

"I haven't told them," Grant said, "and I don't know if Kelli has. I think she should. The last thing Candy needs is an employee being stalked on a catering job by a party crasher, or guests getting caught in a situation where the police have to be called. That would be deadly to a business."

"I agree," Tracy said. "I think Candy should know. I work

for her, and I would feel safer if she knew."

"I'll ask Kelli to tell Candy," Grant said, jumping in his seat as the door to the office opened unexpectedly behind him.

"Tell me what?" Candy asked as she walked into the office carrying a single white envelope.

Tracy said, "A guy who was at the Blalock wedding reception has been harassing and stalking Kelli."

Candy closed the door to the office before taking a seat beside Grant. "Would someone tell me what's going on?"

Grant relayed the same story to Candy that he had just told Tracy.

"This could be dangerous for her and for any guests at an event," Candy said, frowning. "I need to think about this. Unfortunately, we're having to do off-site events while the buildings are being renovated. I need to make some phone calls."

Candy stood and turned to go back to the bakery when she remembered her errand. She handed Tracy the envelope she had been carrying.

"Try this recipe," she said. "If people like it, we can put it in the meals to go." Candy left and went back to the bakery.

Grant got his biscuit and coffee and crossed the street to the bakery's building. On the third floor, Grant walked down the hall to his office. He could hear Kelli on the phone. He was relieved when she started scratching on those wall calendars of hers. That reassured him the call was a client. When the call ended, Grant tapped on her door and opened it.

"Can I come in?" he asked.

"Sure," she said. "What's up?"

Grant closed the door and sat in the chair opposite her.

"Tracy heard that I have a girlfriend named Kelli," he said. "She confronted me about it earlier in the cafe. That news is all over Troy. We were discussing what we could do to help you when Candy came in. She knows, Kelli. She's concerned for you and any guests who happen to be at an event where you're working. She said she was going to make some calls but be prepared for her to confront you. I'm sorry."

"It's okay," Kelli said. "I had decided to tell her today. I just wish I had gotten to do it before she heard it from you. Now I'm afraid she won't trust me."

Grant stood to leave, and Kelli stood, too. "I guess I had better go see her before she comes up here. I can at least do that."

Grant saw dark circles under her eyes giving evidence to the nervousness he knew she was feeling. Her steps were missing their usual bounce and her shoulders were slightly slumped. When Kelli came around the desk, Grant pulled her into a hug.

"It's all going to work out," he said. He released her and said, "Now, go see Candy. I promise she'll be supportive and understanding."

Kelli walked down the stairs then knocked on Candy's office door. Candy was on the phone but motioned for Kelli to come in and pointed to a chair.

"Thanks, Hank," she said. "I'll keep you posted. I appreciate your help," and she ended the call.

"I heard you know my story about Aaron Blalock," Kelli

said. "I'm sorry. I was going to tell you today, honestly, but you heard it before I had the chance."

"I wish you felt you could have trusted us to help you," Candy said. "I know almost everyone in this town, including lawyers and policemen. We can develop a plan to keep you and our customers safe."

"I want you to know," Kelli said, "that if this gets out of hand, I will quit before I put you, employees or guests at risk. I would never want that to happen."

"I believe you," Candy said. "Now, I want to hear the whole thing from you and your perspective."

Kelli spent the next half hour telling Candy every detail. The only thing she left out was the fact that she was afraid she was developing feelings for Grant.

Candy asked, "Have you seen Aaron Blalock since that party?"

"No. Neither has Grant," Kelli replied.

Candy's phone rang.

"Hello," she said. "Hank. Thanks for getting back to me. What did you find?" Candy paused, listening. "Interesting. Are there outstanding warrants for his arrest?" she asked, then listened. "Good. That makes this easy. Thanks. I'll get an event schedule to you as soon as I have it." Candy ended the call and looked at Kelli.

"That was Hank Bowen, the police officer," she said. "I called him and asked him to do some digging on our Aaron Blalock. It turns out that Aaron, son of upstanding citizens in Troy, has some outstanding warrants for his arrest. He has a history of harassing and stalking women. He is also listed as a sex offender."

Kelli felt her face pale.

"I think I'm going to be sick," she said. "Does his family

know?"

"I don't know. If they do, they're keeping it a big secret," Candy replied.

Kelli's eyebrows frowned and her mouth opened in horror.

"All those children and teenage girls at the reception!" Kelli exclaimed. "If his family knew, then they're as bad as he is. I bet Deena has no idea what's going on behind that family's closed doors. What a rude awakening she's going to have."

"I know," Candy said. "I'm going to get the schedule of events for the next few weeks to Hank. Anything in Whitlow can be handled by our police. For anything outside Whitlow, Hank is going to call the local chief of police or sheriff and tell them they might be able to catch a man on the run."

"Aaron is so delusional that I think he believes he's untouchable," Kelli said. "It's creepy."

Candy leaned back in her chair, "One more question."

"Yes?" Kelli asked.

"What's really going on between you and Grant Sparks?" Candy asked, looking at Kelli with her eyebrows raised. "A few weeks ago, you were fighting and couldn't stand each other. Paul and I thought we were going to have to separate you for the sake of both our businesses. Now, you're friends, and he's willing to play at a romance to keep you safe. Will you enlighten me?"

"Honestly, Candy, we're just friends," Kelli said, looking Candy directly in the eye to emphasize the point. "We got past the arguing, and we get along, but we aren't a couple except to try and fool Aaron. I honestly think Grant feels guilty that it's his relative causing problems"

Candy nodded in thought. She had noticed Kelli bite her lip just before she made the friendship comment.

"Just so you know," Candy said, giving Kelli another direct look. "I would not like you to date a fellow employee."

Kelli said, "I understand."

"But Grant is not my employee," Candy replied with a slight grin. "He's Paul's employee. So, there's no conflict. Regardless, I'm glad he's protective of you."

Candy paused then said with a smile, "If you're interested in Grant, go for it. Just avoid bringing drama to the workplace. That's all I ask. I did that enough before Paul and I got married."

Kelli nodded in understanding. When her phone rang, she stood, left the kitchen area to answer it then hurried up to her office.

Aaron stood at the edge of the park watching the street. He had seen a policeman going into the bakery for breakfast, and another got takeout from the café. He had watched Grant cross the street, but he had not seen Kelli. He was going to have to change his view. Maybe the other end of the street or the parking lot behind the bakery would be better.

CHAPTER 17

The next day, the construction noise started. Engineers were watching the crew tear down the brick wall between the two buildings owned by Paul and Candy. A strong support with a thick glass wall and door were going to be put in place on the third floor which would allow access to both buildings from the same elevator. Grant thought he was going crazy. This was worse than Kelli's telephone calls because the noise was constant.

Kelli had escaped to the basement, and Bailey was out of the office. Grant decided to leave the floor as well. He closed his laptop, shut his door and walked down the steps to the first floor. It was much quieter there because the plan was to leave the walls to the bakery intact. That would give the next door retail space security and privacy. Just out of curiosity he went out the back door to see what the back of the building looked like with the construction that was taking place.

While looking at the back wall a movement at the edge of the parking lot caught Grant's attention. Although it was in his peripheral vision, he could tell it was a person. Grant felt the hair on the back of his neck stiffen as if someone was watching him.

Grant pulled his cell phone from his pocket and started taking pictures of the wall and the windows of his office, but he had the camera flipped so it would film what was behind him. When he was sure he had the images he wanted, Grant put the phone back in his pocket and re-entered the building.

Aaron saw Grant taking pictures of the back of the building. He decided it was wise to leave even though he doubted that Grant knew he was nearby. He hesitated when he saw Grant walk back into the building. Good. He could stay, because Kelli's car was parked behind the bakery. If he stayed here long enough, she would come out to go home. Then he could follow her and see where she really lived. He was sure the apartment across the street was Grant's and not hers, because only Grant crossed that street in the mornings. Kelli always drove in from somewhere else.

Standing inside the back entrance next to the stairwell, Grant took his phone and looked through the photos. In one of them, he saw the man that caught his attention. When he enlarged it, Grant felt his stomach drop and anger fill his chest. He had suspected that it might be Aaron, and unfortunately, it was.

Grant walked into Candy's office and said, "You need to call your police friends." He showed her the picture taken behind the building. Then pointing to the man, he said, "That is Aaron Blalock."

Candy stared a moment at the picture, then she picked up the phone and called the police department. She talked with Hank and told him where to find Aaron.

When she ended the call, Candy said, "Go to the basement. Make sure Kelli is there and that she stays in the building until after the police search the area."

Grant ran down the back steps. He ran into the basement calling Kelli's name. She wasn't there. He ran back up the stairs and down the hall to the elevator. He punched the button, planning to check the third floor when he caught a glimpse of a blue dress and strawberry blond hair entering the cafe. Sighing with relief, Grant took his laptop, crossed the street and entered Candy's Café.

Looking around the busy lunch-time crowd, Grant spotted Kelli in Tracy's office. He casually walked through the restaurant to the office, walked in and shut the door. Both women looked at him with surprise.

Grant looked at Kelli and said, "Aaron is behind the bank building." He took his phone from his pocket and showed her the picture.

Kelli paled and put her hand over her mouth as if stifling a scream. She looked at Grant. Grant saw the look of sheer terror in Kelli's eyes and immediately felt protective, wanting to reassure her.

"Candy called the police," Grant said calmly, looking at Kelli. "You are not to go outside. I almost had a panic attack when I couldn't find you in the basement where Candy said you were."

Tracy said, "Kelli, have you told Grant what the police reports say about Aaron?"

"No. I haven't had the chance." Kelli turned to Grant and said, "Candy's friend on the police force searched Aaron's background. There are warrants for his arrest for harassing and stalking women. He has a record and is listed as a sex offender. The police are very interested in finding him."

"I didn't know that," Grant said. "The wedding was the first time I had any contact with him in over ten years. I wonder if his parents know. I almost hope not, because of all those children and teenagers at the wedding reception."

Grant frowned then his eyes suddenly widened.

"I think they know," he said. "A while back they told the family that Aaron had moved away for a job but would eventually be back. I bet he was in prison."

Grant looked at Kelli. "Let's get lunch to go. We can eat upstairs in the apartment where you're out of the way and safe."

"Okay," Kelli said, "but I'm not sure I can eat."

"I'll fix you a salad," Tracy said. "Put it in the fridge until you want it." She got Grant's order and left the office. Before long she was back with the meals in a bag and two drinks.

Grant took the food and ushered Kelli out of the office and through the cafe's back door. In the building's common entryway, they went up the stairs to his apartment. Kelli sat on a stool at the island and put her head in her hands. Grant locked the interior deadbolt on his door then put the food on the counter. He walked over and put his hands on Kelli's shoulders.

"Are you all right?" he asked.

Kelli looked up and said, "No. I'm worried. I'm a little scared, but I'm mostly angry. This guy is an idiot who has ruined other women's lives and now he's trying to ruin mine."

Grant grinned inwardly. He would rather have an angry Kelli than a scared Kelli. Grant walked to the sliding doors to look out onto the street. He took out his phone and called the bakery.

"Candy," he said, "I found Kelli. She's eating lunch with me at my apartment. Would you get her purse and laptop and take them to Tracy at the café? Then I'll get them for her. She can work from here this afternoon since she doesn't have any appointments."

"That's a good idea," Candy replied. "The police searched the area behind the bakery, but they couldn't find Aaron. I'll bring Kelli's purse and laptop."

Frowning, Grant said, "I hate he got away, but thanks for bringing her things over." The call ended.

Grant turned and looked at Kelli.

"By the time the police got to the area behind the building, Aaron had gone, but Candy is bringing your purse and laptop over. She will leave it with Tracy, and I'll go down and get it. You can work from here."

"OK," Kelli said, raising her hands in surrender. "I give up. I'll stay inside and hide until Aaron is found, but only as long as my job isn't jeopardized. If I have an appointment, I'm going across the street."

"Understood," Grant said, nodding. "Tonight, after dark, we're going to go to your apartment where you can pack some clothes. Then you can stay here until Aaron is found. Are you all right with that plan?"

Kelli wanted to jump for joy; she felt safe here. Instead, she rolled her eyes and said, "I guess so. It makes sense."

"Well don't look so happy!" Grant teased. "I might get my feelings hurt. I'm trying to be a good Samaritan here, since it's my cousin and all."

"Sorry," Kelli said with a wry smile. "I appreciate your efforts." She hugged him, "Thank you." Kelli loved the feeling of being in Grant's arms. She wished she could stay there longer, but she broke the hug and said, "Your lunch is getting cold."

Kelli and Grant worked through the afternoon. He was glad Bailey had the on-call tonight.

Just as the sun went down Grant said, "Let's go to your place."

"All right," Kelli said.

They left the apartment and got into Grant's SUV. Arriving at the motel, Kelli was glad she had a first floor set of rooms with a door to the outside of the building. Grant parked at the door. Kelli unlocked the apartment, and they went inside, locking the door behind them. Kelli worked quickly, throwing clothes and toiletries into bags.

She had filled three bags when she said, "This is enough. I have something of everything that I could need at work, pajamas, toiletries, and leisure clothes. I don't need any more."

Grant turned out the lights. They left the rooms, locked the door, and got back into Grant's SUV. He breathed a sigh of relief when they arrived at his apartment without having any contact with Aaron. As he locked the door to the apartment, Grant hoped that Aaron had not seen them and realized where Kelli was staying.

CHAPTER 18

Kelli unpacked her belongings and put them in the dresser and closet of the spare bedroom. She put her toiletries in the bathroom. This was such an unusual situation that she didn't know how to act or feel. Should she be afraid? She was concerned but not shaking in fear. Should she be annoyed at having to leave her home? She might have been if it had not been Grant's apartment where she was staying, especially since it was nicer than her own place. Should she be glad she was spending uninterrupted time with Grant? That answer was a definite yes. With that decided, Kelli walked into the kitchen where Grant was making dinner.

"Can I help?" she asked.

He handed her potatoes that had been boiled in the skin.

"Peel these and cut them into cubes," he instructed.

Kelli did as she was directed. When she was finished, he handed her a boiled egg.

"Peel this and cut it up."

He took the chopped egg and potatoes from her and mixed the two with green pepper and spices then put it in the refrigerator. He handed her a head of broccoli.

"Use half of this and cut it into small spears."

Grant cut two pieces of baked ham and put them on plates. He and Kelli stood in companionable silence as they watched steam envelop the cooking broccoli. When it was ready, Grant put it and the potato salad on the plates.

"It's ready," he said.

"That was fast," Kelli said.

"It was already prepped," he said. "I'm not that good."

While they ate, Grant realized his curtains were open on the sliding glass doors to the balcony. He got up to close them. When he reached for the curtain rod, Grant saw the silhouette of a man leaning arrogantly against a streetlight across the street and looking up at his apartment.

Grant knew it was Aaron. Anger at his cousin and concern for Kelli rushed through his system simultaneously. He jerked the curtains closed then pulled his phone out of his pocket and called the number a police officer had given him in the event he saw Aaron again.

Grant reported the sighting and peeked through the curtains. Aaron was still there. Grant watched as Aaron stood straight and raised two fingers. He pointed first to his eyes then to Grant in a gesture that said he was watching. Then Aaron took both hands and made the classic, stereotypical outline of a female before pointing back to the apartment.

Grant felt his anger rising. He knew Aaron was taunting him, but that didn't change the emotions he was feeling. Grant's gaze moved to the police car that had just turned onto Main Street. When he looked back at Aaron, the man was gone. Grant swore. He shouldn't have taken his eyes off Aaron. Grant called the number again and told the officer that Aaron had left but that he didn't know which way Aaron had gone in the dark.

Aaron smiled as he blended in with the shadows of the alley. He knew Grant had seen him and called the police. Shaking his head with mirth, he wondered when these people would finally realize that he was too smart to be caught.

What made Aaron mad was that he had seen Kelli in the apartment before Grant had closed the curtains. He was sure the apartment was Grant's. That meant Kelli was willingly staying with his cousin. He smiled again as he thought of the different ways that he could punish Kelli when he finally got her alone with him.

Kelli sat at the table watching Grant as he turned away from the curtains.

"He got away again, didn't he," she said.

"Yes," Grant said wearily. "It's no wonder he has evaded arrest for so long, but it won't last forever. He'll make a mistake, and they'll get him."

They cleaned up the kitchen then went into the den.

"Want to watch a movie?" Grant asked.

"Sure. You pick," she said, getting comfortable on the couch.

Grant sat on the couch and turned the channel to a mystery. Even though they thought the plot was good, Grant and Kelli both had difficulty concentrating on the movie. Aaron Blalock kept encroaching on their thoughts.

Kelli felt exhausted from the stress of the day. She yawned, moved closer to Grant and leaned up against his shoulder. Grant noticed her eyes close and her head begin to droop. He pulled her across him holding her head and shoulders in his arms, then leaned his recliner section of the couch back and fell asleep.

Kelli woke to the late-night news. She realized Grant was holding her, and she enjoyed the sensation for as long as she could before she felt him starting to wake up.

Kelli sat up. "Sorry, I didn't realize I had fallen asleep."

"It's okay," he said. "I did, too."

Kelli went to stand, but her foot had gone numb, and she lost her balance. She fell back onto the couch. Grant caught her, pulled her close and kissed her. Kelli wrapped her arms around his neck and kissed him back.

Grant took his time. It was not a light kiss, nor was it a deeply passionate kiss. It was a kiss for the sake of kissing. He shifted her weight on his lap, put his hand on her cheek, and continued to kiss her. When Grant finally broke the kiss, they were both breathing heavily.

"I guess we had better get some sleep," he said as he looked her in the eyes. He gently moved a wayward strand of hair behind her ear. "Who knows what will happen tomorrow."

Kelli nodded but said nothing. She got up and walked to her bedroom. She watched him turn off the lights.

When he started down the hall, she grabbed his hand, stopped him, kissed him quickly and said, "Goodnight." Grant was smiling when he closed the door to his room.

Kelli got ready for bed. She fell asleep smiling.

CHAPTER 19

Kelli woke before her alarm sounded, which was unusual for her. The sun was barely turning the sky blue. She had slept well, but maybe the stress from the day before was affecting her more than she realized. When Kelli walked across the hall to the bathroom, Grant's bedroom door was still closed. She showered, dried her hair, put on her makeup and opened the door. Grant's door was still closed. She stood quietly in the hallway listening, but heard no sound from his room.

Kelli put on a pink sundress with little white flowers scattered across the fabric. The straps crossed in the back and the V neckline dipped showing a small amount of cleavage. Again, a tailored jacket made the dress sharp and professional. She took her purse and laptop to the kitchen and folded her jacket across a dining table chair.

The coffee and coffee filters were sitting on the counter, and Kelli had a pot of coffee brewing in a few minutes. While waiting for the coffee, Kelli opened her laptop and reviewed the requests from the client she was meeting this morning at ten o'clock. She retrieved a notepad from her briefcase and made a list of items she needed to get from the basement. She wanted the client to have several choices of colors and decorations.

Kelli was concentrating when she heard Grant walking down the hall to the kitchen.

She looked up and said, "Good morning."

"Good morning," Grant said. He grinned mischievously, "You look better this morning than the last morning you were here."

"Don't remind me," Kelli said, rolling her eyes. "I was a mess."

Grant laughed and started to speak when Kelli's phone rang.

"Cotton Catering and Events." Kelli paused. "Yes, Ma'am. I will see you at ten. Thank you." She ended the call.

"You're going to work?" Grant asked, "I thought we agreed that you would stay here."

"I said I would be glad to stay if I didn't have any appointments. I have one today," she said.

Grant started to protest but Kelli stopped him.

"I've already called Tracy. She's going to let me know when a policeman is downstairs getting breakfast so I can get him to walk me across the street." She looked at Grant. "Policemen have weapons and radios. See? Safe." Kelli gave him a grin and a wink.

Grant looked skeptical but agreed. He poured a cup of coffee and opened a Danish he had pulled from the pantry.

Kelli took a bite, "This is good, but not as good as Candy's."

"I know. I have one of hers in the freezer, but I forgot to put it out to thaw last night," Grant said.

They had just finished eating and washing their dishes when Kelli's phone rang.

"Cotton Catering and Events." She listened then said, "Thanks. I'm on my way." Kelli closed her laptop and put it in her bag. She put on the jacket then picked up her purse and bag.

"The officer is downstairs and ready to escort me," Kelli told Grant. "Are you coming or do you need to finish getting ready?"

"I'll walk you down, but I still have a few things to do here." Grant walked Kelli to the café and turned her over to the policeman's care. He said, "See you later,"

Kelli waved bye and turned the police officer. "I've seen you in the bakery," she said, looking at his name badge. "Officer Jones. I appreciate your doing this."

"Call me Mark," he said, "and I'm glad to help you out."

Mark stopped outside the cafe door. He looked up and down the street, then said, "Okay. Let's go."

"What did you get for breakfast?" Kelli asked as they stepped onto the curb outside the bakery.

"A sausage biscuit," he answered, holding up a white to-go bag with a small amount of grease bleeding through the paper. He opened the bakery door for Kelli and scanned the street behind them as she walked into the building.

When he walked into the bakery behind her, Kelli said, "Ellen, can I have one of those bear claws?" She filled a cup with coffee from a row of decanters along the wall of the sitting area. She handed it and the bear claw to the officer.

"Thank you," Kelli said. "I really do appreciate you for walking across the street with me."

"My pleasure," Officer Jones said, smiling at her as he left the bakery.

Kelli paid Ellen for the pastry, got a cup of coffee and rode the elevator up the stairs. She had put everything in place for her appointment when Grant walked down the hall and stopped in the doorway to her office.

"Looks good," he said, nodding with approval as he looked around. "You haven't forgotten a thing."

"How would you know?" Kelli asked as she burst into laughter. "Have you ever catered a reception?"

"No," Grant answered smiling, "but I know how thorough you are."

In the lobby Bailey rolled her eyes as flirtatious laughter echoed down the hallway. She almost wished they were still fighting.

The appointment was over, decisions were made, and Kelli held the check for the down payment in her hand. She went down the back stairs and into the kitchen where Candy pulled a tray of cookies out of the oven.

"I know where to put it," Kelli said, waving the check in the air and heading to the filing cabinet behind Candy's desk.

"Those smell wonderful!" Kelli exclaimed as she came out of the office. "Are those pumpkin cookies?"

"Yes," Candy replied. "I'm getting a head start on Halloween. I'll freeze these then thaw and decorate them before the Halloween carnival upstairs. I'm guessing you had a successful appointment?"

"Yes," Kelli said. " We're just providing food. They're using the fellowship hall at the Baptist Church. It's not until November, but we don't have to worry about construction on the second floor. They're even doing their own decorations."

"Easy. I like that," Candy said.

"Well, they want fancy cupcakes for dessert," Kelli said as she handed Candy a piece of paper with the date of the dinner. Five dozen cupcakes of assorted flavors and decorations had been ordered.

"Okay," Candy said, "I prefer it when they want everything alike. Less time consuming."

"I can imagine," Kelli said. "I'm going back upstairs. I will prep everything for my appointment tomorrow then go back to Grant's. We've gotten two events from the website I started a month ago, so I think it's working well. I'll update that this afternoon."

"All right. Just be safe, wherever you decide to work from," Candy said.

Kelli walked back up the stairs to the third floor. She gathered her samples and prepared for her appointment the next day. When she was finished, she tapped on Grant's door.

"Come in," he said.

Kelli opened the door.

Grant smiled when he saw who it was. "How did the appointment go?"

"Good. I'm finished here if you want to go back across the street," she said.

"OK. I need to finish this and close out the file. It should only take about five more minutes. I'll come get you."

"Sounds like a plan," Kelli replied and walked back to her office.

In less than five minutes Grant stood at her door. "Ready to go?"

Kelli picked up her purse and the bag with her computer. "Yep. Let's go."

Kelli stood inside the building door while Grant checked the street.

He opened the door and said, "I don't see him. Let's go."

The two walked across the street without incident. Inside the café they ordered lunch to go.

Aaron sat on a bench in the shadows of deep shade at the edge of the park. He watched Kelli and Grant cross the street and enter the café. He was frustrated. Grant was keeping Kelli from him, and family or not, he was going to have to deal with him. Unfortunately, the city police were always patrolling Main Street.

Grant unlocked the door to his apartment and pushed the door open so Kelli could go in ahead of him. Kelli placed her food on the counter and took her belongings to her bedroom. She put her computer bag on the bed then removed her shoes and jacket and put them in the closet. Walking back into the kitchen, she took her food and sat at the kitchen island to eat. She made a deep sigh.

"What's wrong?" Grant asked as he placed his food beside hers and sat on the barstool.

"I should be across the street working. I need to re-organize the basement. I need to make plans and brain-storm new ideas and themes. Instead, I'm hiding out in an apartment watching the place where I need to be. It's just frustrating."

Grant stepped behind Kelli and started kneading the muscles in her neck and shoulders.

"Relax," he said. "Your muscles are in knots."

Kelli started to relax. "Umm, that feels so good."

Grant continued massaging her muscles. He gradually moved his hands down her neck, to her shoulders, to her upper back. As he continued massaging her neck and shoulders, he felt Kelli was relaxing.

Kelli was feeling so relaxed she could barely keep her head up. She closed her eyes, enjoying the massage as Grant worked the knots out of her muscles. She felt Grant's hands across her back, shoulders, and neck. She delighted in the way they made her feel, safe and relaxed.

Kelli's phone rang and brought a halt to Grant's massage on her shoulders. She stood and walked back to the bedroom where she had left her phone.

Taking it and her laptop back to the kitchen, she answered, "Cotton Catering and Events."

She listened then said, "Yes, I would love to meet with you to discuss a date and details for your event." She looked at the phone on her calendar, "Can you come tomorrow?" Kelli listened. "What time would you like to meet?" She paused, listening. "That's fine with me. Do you know where our office is?" She paused again. "Correct. Just come up to the third floor, go down the hall, and I'm in the office on the right. I look forward to seeing you tomorrow." Kelli ended the call. Kelli sat at the island making notes on on the computer when her stomach growled.

"I guess we had better eat lunch," Grant said with a grin and pointed to her lunch still sitting at her place. "Eat," and he opened his own lunch and took a bite.

Kelli was hungry, and a grilled chicken salad had never tasted so good. She looked at Grant, smiled, and ate with fervor. Grant smiled. He was happy she was relaxed and smiling.

When Grant and Kelli had finished lunch, they opened their laptops and worked at the dining room table. Grant felt the need to work in the same space as Kelli. While he knew they were safe in the apartment, the need to just make sure everything was all right overshadowed using the comfortable chair at the desk in his bedroom. They worked in silence, each with his or her own agenda.

Kelli broke the silence.

"When you finish what you're doing, will you critique my website and social media page for the company?" she asked.

"Sure. Hand me the laptop." Grant held the computer and scrolled through the sites.

"Your social media page is great with lots of pictures, contact information, list of services. I wouldn't change anything except to add pictures." He then showed her how to change things on the website to make it more user friendly.

"Oh, my!" she said. "That does make it easier. Thanks."

"You're welcome," Grant replied, smiling.

A timer sounded in the kitchen. Grant looked at his watch and saw that it was five o'clock. He closed his laptop, stood and walked to the kitchen to start dinner.

Kelli joined him and asked, "What can I do?"

Grant handed her vegetables.

"Make a salad," he said.

Grant took a large steak from the refrigerator and cut it in half. He placed it on the grill at the back of the stove top and started a low heat. He melted some butter, added garlic and spices and brushed the top of the steaks. He turned them over and brushed the other side then raised the heat. Then he sliced a loaf of Italian bread, spread butter and garlic over the slices and placed them in the oven. When everything was done, he got the leftover potato salad from the refrigerator, plated the food and took it to the island. Kelli made drinks and joined him.

They talked about their jobs, their college experiences, Whitlow, favorite foods, movies and TV shows. They avoided the subject of Aaron. Both felt the change in their relationship, but neither wanted to talk about it.

When the kitchen was cleaned Kelli asked, "Would you mind if I took a bath in your tub?"

"Help yourself," Grant replied watching her.

"Thank you," she replied with a grateful smile.

Kelli walked to her bedroom to gather her toiletries and a change of clothes. In Grant's bathroom she ran hot water into the tub. Finding towels, she placed them on the tile beside the porcelain, took off her clothes and climbed into the tub. Kelli leaned her head back against the curve of the porcelain and sighed. For the first time in over a week, she felt relaxed. Warm water moved around her, soothing tense muscles, and the subtle scent of lavender calmed her frayed nerves. Kelli closed her eyes. The knock on the bathroom door jolted her back to reality.

"Yes?" she called.

"Just checking," Grant called through the door. "You've been in there a long time. I didn't want you to fall asleep and drown."

"I'm getting out. The water has cooled." Kelli dried off and put on her pajama shorts and t shirt. She walked into the den where Grant sat on the couch. A baseball game was played with no sound on the TV.

Kelli sat down on the couch and said, "That was wonderful. Thank you. I feel like my muscles have relaxed into butter."

"Good," Grant said, smiling. "It's not late, anything you want to watch on TV?"

"No. Not really." Kelli snuggled up against Grant and watched the baseball game until it was time to go to bed.

CHAPTER 20

Kelli woke up for the third time during the night. It was still dark, and the beams of a streetlight made their way through the curtain across the window. Her phone sat on the side table, and she checked the time. It was only four am. She could still sleep another two hours, but that would depend on whether or not she could get back to sleep. She was sure her inability to stay asleep had something to do with the stress Aaron Blalock was causing her. It made her mad that he could get into her mind so thoroughly that her rest was disrupted.

Later, bright sunlight streamed through the window, landing on Kelli's eyes. She groggily reached for her phone, wondering what time it was and heard Grant knocking on her door.

"I thought you had an appointment this morning," he called out.

Grant's statement hit her like a bucket of cold water.

"Oh my gosh! I forgot!" Kelli exclaimed, sitting straight up in bed. She jumped up and ran across the hall to the bathroom. He watched her run back across the hall and grab items she had forgotten and run back into the bathroom.

"Take it easy," Grant said, laughing. "It's only seven. Your appointment isn't for three hours."

Grant was already dressed, and he walked down the hall to start coffee in the kitchen. When he heard Kelli drying her hair in the bathroom, Grant took the raspberry muffins he had bought from Candy the day before from the refrigerator. They would microwave well.

He was drinking a cup of coffee when Kelli came into the kitchen. She wore a pale sage green sleeveless dress that had a high neck and a ruffle that tickled her chin. Grant noticed that the color made the light red highlights in her blonde hair more noticeable.

"That's different," he said, pointing to the ruffle at her neck.

"Just one in the wardrobe," she said as she poured a cup of coffee. "Are you going to go with me across the street or do I need to find a police officer."

"I can walk you over," he said. "Although I bet the officers at the police department are drawing straws to see which one gets to escort the beautiful Kelli Mills across the street, especially when she gives them coffee and pastries."

"You think?" Kellli asked with a laugh. "I have no doubt that they would all compete for the bear claws and coffee."

The two were just getting ready to go downstairs when Tracy called telling her there was a police officer waiting for her. Kelli told her she would be right down. When she ended the call, she burst into laughter.

"What?" Grant asked.

Kelli took a deep breath. "There's a police officer

downstairs waiting to escort me across the street."

Grant grinned, "Told ya." He took her hand and said, "Before we go, we need to decide something. I think we can agree that we have crossed the line from just friends to two people exploring the possibility of a relationship. You are going to be a huge distraction for me but for a different reason than when you first arrived. Do we act like we are a couple, or do we keep a cool, professional tone?"

Kelli thought for a moment.

"I say the cool professional tone. Candy warned me to not bring drama into the workplace if I started seeing you for real," she said.

"Okay," he said. "Distant and professional. I can do that." Grant paused then with a grin said, "Maybe."

Kelli smiled as she walked downstairs ahead of Grant while he locked the door. When she entered the café, she saw a different officer from the day before.

He jumped up from a stool at the counter, "Miss Mills, I'm here to get you safely across the street."

Kelli smiled and said, "Lead the way."

They were halfway across the street by the time Grant entered the café. He looked confused.

"Where did she go?" he asked Tracy.

Tracy, who was standing behind the counter collecting dirty dishes, pointed to the street.

"That boy has been fidgeting for five minutes waiting for her," she said.

Grant looked out the cafe door to see Kellie's blond hair and green dress crossing the street. The young police office kept scanning the street until they reached the bakery's door.

"It's the bear claws and coffee," Grant said with a chuckle.

"Well, that's part of it, I'm sure," Tracy said, "but they all salivate over her."

"I know," Grant replied. "She handles it well, though. She's kind enough to not embarrass them. I'll give her credit for that."

Tracy stopped wiping the counter and looked at him.

"So, you two are friends now?" she asked.

Grant shrugged. "Considering we have to fake a relationship, I guess so."

Tracy rolled her eyes, "Fake? Come on, you two dance around each other like two birds waiting to mate. Give it up and go for it. She's a nice person."

Grant looked across the street where Kelli had already disappeared into the building.

"I don't know," he said. "We'll see. We both worked around the same table for a few hours yesterday without talking or arguing. That's a start."

"There you go," Tracy said.

Kelli was already in her office working when Grant walked onto the third floor. Bailey came through the door to the stairwell as he was walking down the hall.

"Bailey," he said. "When you get settled in, come back to my office. I want to get your opinion on a few things."

"Sure," she said. "I'll be right there." Bailey came back down the hall as he was laying out papers on his desk.

Kelli heard them talking, but she tuned them out to display her samples on the table for her client. Mrs. Freedman arrived promptly at ten. Kelli made her comfortable, asked what she had in mind, then gave her examples of her choices.

An hour later, she and Mrs. Freedman had a plan, and Kelli had a down payment. She emailed the information to Tracy and Candy then took the check downstairs. Candy was in the kitchen decorating cookies.

"Cute," Kelli said, looking over Candy's shoulder. "Lay a couple out for me to get a picture." Candy obliged her.

"The holidays aren't too far off," Kelli said. "My latest booking is already in December. Can you get me a list of the different holiday specialties you can provide?"

"Sure," Candy said. She looked closely at Kelli.

"How are you doing?" Candy asked, setting down her piping bag. "It's got to be stressful having your life turned upside down and your activity curtailed because you're being stalked by a convicted sex offender."

Kelli rolled her eyes and turned up a lip.

"It's the pits," she answered. "I hate not being able to do what I want when I want. I hate feeling like I need to look over my shoulder. I just want the guy caught."

Candy looked at Kelli seriously and said, "I'm angry at the police. They want to use you as bait to lure Aaron out of hiding. A representative from the police departments in Greensboro and Charlotte are here. They have warrants for his arrest. Evidently the guy gets around."

"Two big cities?" Kelli asked, shocked. She grimaced, "Yuck. He really is a sick creep."

"Hank has been keeping me informed," Candy said. "According to the other officers, Aaron has never stalked one woman this long. They think it's because of Grant. They think he is competing with Grant for you."

"That's ridiculous and a little sleezy." Kelli gave an involuntary shiver and looked worried. "Does this put

Grant in danger? I mean, if Aaron thinks Grant is competition, how far would he go to eliminate that competition?"

"I'm sure the police have thought of that aspect and several others," Candy said. "Hank would let me know if we had anything to be worried about."

Kelli thought for a moment.

"I'm going upstairs to talk with Grant," she said. "The last thing I want to do is put anyone in danger. I love this job and Whitlow, but I will leave town before I do that." Kelli left the kitchen and climbed the back stairs to the third floor.

The door to the stairwell on the third floor opened, and Kelli walked through to the hallway. She started to go to Grant's office, but she heard him still talking with Bailey. She turned and went to her own office. It sounded like he was giving Bailey more responsibility. Good for her.

Eventually Bailey walked back down the hall to her desk. Kelli got up and went to Grant's office. She tapped on the door frame. Grant looked up, surprised.

"Can I come in?" Kelli asked.

"Of course." He motioned for her to sit on the couch along the wall. She did. He sat beside her, gave her a big smile.

"To what do I owe the pleasure of your company?" he asked.

"Aaron." Kelli said.

"What's he done now?" Grant asked, frowning.

"Nothing yet," Kelli replied. "Candy said law enforcement representatives from Charlotte and Greensboro have come to Whitlow looking for Aaron. They think he's escalating and that he may be competing with you to get to me."

"That's an interesting theory," Grant said. "If that's true, then making him think we are a couple has backfired. It made him more determined."

"Exactly," Kelli said. "My concern is that if he sees you as competition, he will resort to anything to get you out of the picture. You may be the one in danger here, not me. You saw him watching your apartment, so he knows where I am. It's only a matter of time before he becomes brave enough to act. I don't want his first course of action to be harming you."

Grant played with the fingers on her right hand.

"Don't worry about me," he said. "I can be resourceful when I need to be. I just don't want him to hurt you. Are you finished here for the day?"

"Almost," she said. "I need to spend some time rummaging through the basement to see if I need to order any extra chair covers for the event that I scheduled this morning. It's a large reception at the Troy Senior Center."

Grant frowned, "How long will you be down there?"

"I don't know, maybe five minutes, maybe an hour," she replied. "It just depends on what I find."

Grant stood, picking up his laptop and some paper.

"I'll go with you," he said. "I can enter this data down there as easily as I can up here. The basement can be entered through the elevator or stairs. I would feel better if you weren't alone."

"You really don't have to," Kelli said, "but I'm not going to argue with you about it. Are you ready to go now?"

"Lead the way," Grant said.

Kelli and Grant took the stairs to the basement. Grant sat at the table Kelli had turned into a makeshift desk and started inputting his data. Kelli started rummaging through the cabinets. Eventually, she found all the white chair covers and put them on a table for counting. Grant had completely tuned her out and continued working.

Chair covers in stacks of ten were collecting on the table when Kelli heard the elevator open. She looked up, and Candy walked into the basement.

"I hoped you'd be down here," she said. "I checked your office first." Candy looked at Grant in surprise, "What are you doing here, Grant?"

He gave a wry grin and said, "Just fulfilling my duties as Knight in Shining Armor."

Candy gave him a look that said, "Yeah, right. Tell me another fib."

"No, really," Grant said, "I just didn't want her to be alone down here. I can work anywhere. She counts quietly."

Kelli rolled her eyes at Candy and shook her head.

"Grant seems to think he needs to account for my every move. All because my stalker is his cousin," Kelli said.

"I feel responsible," Grant said. "I'm the one that introduced him to you. Reluctantly, but still, I did."

Candy said to Kelli, "Well, I was looking for you to give you this. It's the list of holiday specialties available from October through New Year's. The price is good through November first. After that I need to reevaluate the costs."

"This is amazing," Kelli said as she looked through the stack of papers. "When you start cooking, I want pictures. The website will go viral with these." Kelli looked at Candy with a grin, "We should start a channel on YouTube. You can teach how to decorate cookies and cakes."

"Uh, no," Candy said. "Pictures on a website and social media are fine. No videos. I can't even stand up and speak in front of the Sunday School class. There's no way I could for a camera."

"Well, we could try one informally, knowing it won't go on the internet and just see how you do. You talk in front of a class at the community college," Kelli said.

"That's different. I'm teaching," Candy replied.

"See, that's what I'm talking about," Kelli said, pointing to Candy. "You'll be teaching on camera, not in person. Just think about it."

Candy blew out a breath. "OK. I'll think about it."

Kelli grinned, clapped, and squeaked, "Yay."

Candy turned, "I'm leaving." She pointed to the chair covers, "Order what you need. When it's over we can cull the ones that are torn or stained."

"Yes, boss," Kelli said with a salute.

Chapter 21

Grant escorted Kelli across the street from the bakery. They stopped in the café long enough to order lunch then took it upstairs. Kelli carried the food to the kitchen island while Grant locked the door behind them.

"I'm going to change," Kelli said as she walked into her bedroom. She came out ten minutes later in a pair of shorts, a tank top, and a lightweight cardigan sweater that was open in the front. She sat beside Grant at the island, then noticed him watching her.

"What?" she asked, pulling her food closer.

"Woman, you make it very difficult to concentrate on anything but the way you look. How is it that you look amazing no matter what you wear?" he asked.

Kelli smiled, leaned over and kissed him. "Thank you. That was a lovely compliment."

Grant grabbed Kelli by the waist and pulled her over onto his lap. He kissed her. Kelli put her arms around his neck and kissed him back. Grant began to deepen the kiss when Kelli's phone rang.

"Ugh!" Grant groaned. "Turn that thing off!"

Kelli giggled, jumped off Grant's lap and walked to

the counter to pick up the phone. "Cotton Catering and Events."

Grant tuned out Kelli's conversation and started to eat. He felt Kelli grab his arm. When he looked up, Kelli's face was pale and her hand shook as she placed the phone on the island and put it on speaker.

"Kelli, I know where you are," Aaron's voice said from the phone. "Don't think I'm not aware of what you're doing. You're cheating on me, and it makes me angry. Do you know what I do when I am angry?"

Kelli watched Grant get out his own phone. She wasn't sure what he intended until she saw him press the record button and place the phone on the island next to hers.

"No Aaron," she said, "What do you do when you're angry?"

"That depends on just how mad I am," Aaron told her. "The last time you made me mad, I locked you up for two days, remember? How can you forget being locked up for two days in total darkness with no one to talk to?"

Kelli looked at Grant in horror. She hesitated for a moment.

"Where were we when you did that?" she asked, sounding confused. "I'm not sure I remember. Are you sure it was me?"

"Well, let me refresh your memory," Aaron said. "I found you cheating all the way over in Greensboro. Remember that?"

"Why was I in Greensboro, Aaron?" Kelli asked. Grant was still recording the call with his phone, but he reached into her purse to get her personal phone. He used it to call the police.

"You know why, slut!" Aaron shouted angrily. "You were

cheating. I had to teach you a lesson."

Kelli flattened her hands on the island and fought back the bile that rose in her throat.

"How did you teach me a lesson, Aaron?" she asked shakily.

"Focus, Kelli," Aaron said, sounding annoyed. "We had gone to my cabin at the lake. I locked you in the basement for two days, remember? Remember?"

"Did I learn my lesson?" she asked.

"I thought so. I knew you would never cheat again, but look at what you're doing now, and with my cousin. That makes me real mad, Kelli. You don't cheat on me with family."

"Where are you now, Aaron?" she asked.

"I'm right outside your door, slut," he said in a threatening voice.

Kelli looked at Grant in horror. Grant was standing near his apartment door talking softly to the police using Kelli's phone. When he heard what Aaron said, he rechecked the interior bolt and told the police to come to his apartment.

"Aaron, can we talk about this?" Kelli answered.

"No," Aaron said firmly. "It's too late. I'm done talking. I'm going to teach my cousin a lesson, then I am going to teach you a lesson," Kelli heard the wail of sirens coming from the street.

"What did you do, Kelli?" Aaron asked. "Did you call the police? They won't find me because I'm too slippery, but I'll find you. I know where you are." Aaron ended the call abruptly.

Grant stopped the recording on his phone. He spoke into Kelli's phone again. A knock came at Grant's door. He spoke one more time into Kelli's phone then opened the door. Hank Bowen came into the apartment.

Grant played the recording from his phone for Hank, and Hank asked him to message it to his phone. Hank looked over at Kelli. Grant followed his eyes.

Kelli was sitting on the stool. Her feet were pulled up to the seat, and she had her arms wrapped around her legs. Her chin rested on her knees. She said nothing, just stared into space.

Grant got up, walked to her and placed a hand on her shoulders.

"Kelli?" he asked. "Are you all right?"

Kelli had been so scared that she momentarily froze, but fright turned to anger. She looked up, lowered her feet, then turned and looked at Hank.

"You need to get that creep," she said defiantly. "Was the story about a woman in Greensboro true? Did he do that to a woman over there?"

"According to all the reports and outstanding warrants I've read about Aaron," Hank said, "that has not been mentioned. So far, no woman in Greensboro has reported being abducted and locked up by him."

"I want this over," Kelli said. "I'm ready to plan a trap to catch him, and I volunteer as bait. Hank, you and the others plan it and let me know what I'm supposed to do."

Grant objected. "There has to be another way to catch Aaron without putting Kelli in danger. Hank, you and the others can figure out how you're going to catch Aaron without Kelli."

Kelli glared at Grant.

"Aaron is an evil slippery eel who is completely delusional and obsessed," she said. "The only way he's going to come out of the slime and expose himself is if I'm dangled on the hook for him to take a bite. Anything else is just going to drag this out, and I am tired of putting my life on hold because of a sleezy scumbag.

Grant started to speak again when Hank said, "All right, I'll go back to the department and discuss this with the chief, the sheriff's department, and the officers from the other cities who want him as badly as we do. I'll let you know what we decide."

Grant walked Hank to the door and locked it when the officer had gone.

He turned and looked at Kelli.

"I don't want you to underestimate Aaron," he said. "The one thing I remember about Aaron as a kid is that he is very manipulative. He would create all sorts of mischief. Everyone knew he was the culprit, but he never got caught. Plus, his parents always got him out of trouble. Let the professionals make their plans and catch him."

Kelli was angry. Everyone seemed to think they knew what was best for her. She was tired of hiding, tired of putting her job and her life on hold, and she finally admitted to herself that she was scared. That last phone call cut through every defense she had and scared her.

When Kelli admitted to herself that she was scared, she sighed, feeling the anger leave. She looked at Grant.

"Okay. Let's wait and hear their plans." She heard Grant sigh with relief.

Kelli picked up her salad and put it in the refrigerator.

"I'm not hungry," she said. "Maybe later."

Grant watched Kelli walk over to the sofa, take the soft blanket off the back of the cushions, then sit in the corner of the cushions with the blanket around her. He could tell she was upset, most likely scared. Without saying a word, Grant followed her to the couch. He sat down and pulled her into his arms. They just sat there, Kelli curled up against Grant, and Grant holding her close.

"Want to talk about it?" he asked.

"I'm angry, frustrated, bewildered and scared all at the same time," Kelli replied. "I don't know how to feel or what to do."

"I get that," Grant said. "I'm angry and frustrated myself, and I'm worried about you." Grant kissed the top of Kelli's head. "I just want to keep you safe." Grant smiled, "Well, that and kiss you."

Kelli smiled, turned her face up and kissed him.

"I can live with that," she said, smiling.

Aaron walked back to his car. He was furious. Kelli had called the police. She would have to be punished. And that useless cousin, Grant, had probably encouraged it. Aaron was tired of Grant getting in his way. It was past time he dealt with his annoying relative. He would find a way to get to them. They couldn't keep hiding forever, and he was a very patient man. Aaron smiled to himself. Yes, he was very patient. They would make a mistake, and he would be waiting for them. Take Grant out, and Kelli was his.

*****

Hank Bowen played the recording of Kelli's conversation with Aaron to the police officers gathered at his office. He looked at the officer from Greensboro.

"Did he kidnap a woman in Greensboro?" Hank asked.

"He was sent to prison for multiple accounts of stalking, breaking and entering, harrassment, and indecent exposure, the Greensboro officer replied. "He hasn't been accused of kidnapping since he got out of prison, but there are several missing persons that have been reported since he was released. One is a friend to the woman who reported him last time, which is why we're so interested in him. If what he said is true, he could be a murderer as well as a sex offender. And if he has murdered, he won't hesitate to do so again. I think he would kill Grant to get to Kelli, who is his latest obsession."

The police officer from Charlotte said, "Blalock is a person of interest in a report of stalking. He was seen in the neighborhood where there have been a rash of break-ins, all apartments of women in their twenties. Nothing was stolen, but the victims found their lingerie removed from a drawer and arranged on a bed. His fingerprints were in one apartment. We have him on camera approaching women in several bars downtown. He followed one woman all the way to her car. "

Bob Sanders, Chief of Police in Whitlow, said, "I'm calling the State Bureau of Investigation. I think this qualifies for their involvement. He has outstanding warrants in multiple cities and is a possible murderer, even serial killer." He left the conference room, went to his office and made the phone call.

CHAPTER 22

That afternoon, Kelli and Grant sat working at the dining area when Kelli's phone rang.

"Hello?"

"Miss Mills, this is Bob Sanders, Chief of Police here in Whitlow. Is Mr. Sparks with you?"

"Yes," Kelli answered.

"Would you put your phone on speaker so we can all talk?" he asked.

Kelli tapped a button on her phone then said, "You're on speaker, Mr. Sanders."

"I just wanted the two of you to know that the police departments of Greensboro and Charlotte plus the SBI are represented in Whitlow," Sanders told them. "We have devised a plan to lure Aaron Blalock out into the open. I don't want to give you the details because I want you to act naturally. Would the two of you please go across the street to your offices as if you are going to work?"

"Yes," Kelli answered. "We can do that."

"Good. Hank Bowen will go into the bakery like he usually does," Chief Sanders continued, "only this time he will have some equipment for you. I need you to wear small radios in your ears so we can give you directions. Can you do that?"

"Yes. We'll go there now," Kelli said and ended the call.

"What do you think they're going to do?" she asked Grant.

"I guess we'll find out," he said. "Let's pack up the computers. We need to make this look real."

Kelli nodded in agreement, shut her computer down and placed it in her work bag. Grant did the same and placed his laptop in a briefcase.

Kelli changed back into her work clothes to give the appearance of continuing her workday. When they were ready, Kelli and Grant followed their usual route through the café. At the door Grant looked up and down the street then led Kelli across to the bakery.

Candy looked up in surprise when she saw Kelli and Grant coming through the front door. She looked at the clock. It was the usual slow time for the bakery. People would start coming in around four o'clock to pick up orders for cakes or the meals-to-go.

"I thought you were finished here for the day," she said.

"Hank Bowen is coming. Evidently the police have a plan, and he's bringing us some equipment," Kelli said.

Candy looked concerned. "What type of plan?"

"I have no idea," Kelli replied. "I guess we'll find out when Hank gets here. I think we need to go up to the offices like we're working. Will you let us know when he comes into the bakery?"

"Of course," Candy said. She frowned as she watched the two get on the elevator and go to the third floor.

On the third floor Grant said, "Come to my office and work there, or we can go down to the basement if you need to organize and plan in your space."

"Do you mind if we go to the basement?" Kelli asked.

"No." Grant opened the elevator doors and pushed the button for the basement. When the doors were closed, he pulled Kelli into his arms. He held her tight and rested his cheek against her head.

"I don't like this, Kelli," he said softly, "but I don't think we have a choice."

"I know," Kelli said. "But offense is better than defense. I'm glad we're being proactive instead of waiting around for Aaron to decide what to do. That's even scarier for me."

Grant started working on his computer while Kelli straightened and organized the contents of the basement. She had been so busy with events and appointments that she had not had time to properly put things back in place. An hour later, the basement door opened, and Officer Hank Bowen entered.

"Sorry it took so long," he said as he sat at the table. "Candy thought you two were upstairs, so I checked there first. I figured this was the only other place you could work in this building."

"Sorry," Kelli said, nervously biting her lip. "I should have told her."

Hank had two small boxes. He slid them across the table, one to Kelli and one to Grant. Inside was a small radio disguised as a hearing aid that would not be noticeable once it was inside the ear canal.

"Put it in your ear," Hank said. Hank watched the couple put the radios in their ears. He noticed Kelli's hands were trembling slightly. Grant appeared calm. Hank then made a call on his cell phone.

"Ready for testing," he said.

Kelli and Grant were getting used to the way the radio felt inside their ears when they suddenly heard static. Then they each heard a voice.

"Kelli, Grant, if you can hear me say yes."

Grant said, "Yes."

Kelli said, "Yes."

"Good. This is Chief Sanders. I want you to keep these radios in their boxes. Tomorrow morning, I need you two to go running in the park at exactly seven o'clock with the radios in your ears. There will be plainclothes officers in the park keeping watch over you. If we need you to do anything different from running, we will let you know through the radios. Act like it is a normal exercise outing for you. Talk normally, stop and walk occasionally, then run. Do this for half an hour then go sit on the bench on Main Street at the park entrance. Just sit and have a casual conversation. Look at your watches like you need to get ready for work, then go back to the apartment. I will call you there."

"Okay," Kelli said. "We can do that."

"Thank you," Sanders said. "We have eyes on the street and your apartment. Act like this is a normal day. Kelli, you need to look slightly nervous. Grant, you hold Kelli's arm and look protective as you go back across the street. I want you both to have dinner in the café tonight at six. When you are finished eating, go outside like you are going to take an evening stroll. Go down a few doors, stop, act nervous, change your mind and go back to your apartment. Stay there until morning. If anything changes, either I or Officer Bowen will let you know. Do you understand everything?"

Grant locked eyes with Kelli, his eyebrows raising in question. Kelli gave him a slight smile and nodded.

"Yes," Kelli said. "We understand."

"Good," Chief Sanders said. "You can take the radios out of your ears. Just remember to put them in tomorrow morning."

After a moment of silence on the radio, Kelli and Grant took the devices from their ears. They put them back in the box that had a charging station and cord.

"Any questions?" Hank asked.

"No," Kelli said.

"I have one," Grant said. "Can you assure me that Kelli is going to be safe if we do this?"

Hank smiled. "If you knew the number of officers that have come into town in the last few hours, you wouldn't even have that question. There are at least six watching this building and the café right now. They want this guy. His psychological profile suggests he is escalating, and they don't know what he will do. They definitely want him in custody before he has a chance to commit another crime."

"Okay," Grant said, nodding. "We'll follow the plan."

"Thanks. I'll keep in touch," Hank said. He stood up from the table and left the basement.

Grant watched Hank leave the basement. He looked over at Kelli who had her head down, staring intently at the box with the radio inside.

"Are you okay?" he asked.

Kelli looked at him and nodded.

"I won't need to put on a nervous act," she said. "I've

been mad at Aaron, but I don't think I realized how serious this was until today. That phone call. These radios. This is scary stuff."

Grant put his arm around Kelli.

"I know, but you heard Hank say how many police officers there are on this. You'll be fine," Grant said, trying to sound more confident than he felt.

"Let's get back to the apartment," Kelli said. "If I'm going to be an actress, I want to look my best."

"Don't go too overboard with that," Grant said with a frown.

"According to the plan, I'll be dressing up for you," Kelli said with a grin. "Don't go getting all snippy thinking I'm dressing for Aaron." Grant laughed when Kelli's grin turned to a grimace.

Kelli looked at Grant with a question in her eyes.

"What?" he asked.

Kelli whispered, "Do you think they can hear us even if we don't have the radios in our ears?"

Grant looked surprised and whispered back, "I never thought of that." He grinned. "We need to place them next to the TV and keep it on all evening. We may not want anyone to hear us talking or doing this." Grant pulled Kelli to him and kissed her.

Kelli giggled. "No. We don't want that," she said and kissed him back.

Candy watched as Grant and Kelli opened the stairwell door and walked into the lobby.

"Well?" she asked. "What's the plan?"

"We don't know everything," Grant said. "We're to eat at the café at six tonight and go running in the morning."

"That's it?" Candy asked incredulously. "No more information?"

Kelli shrugged, "I'm supposed to act nervous at times, but other than that, they want us to act naturally. We'll get more instructions tomorrow."

"I don't like this," Candy said. "That man is dangerous."

"Hank said they have extra help in the area for now," Grant said and looked at his watch. "Don't worry until you have to. We need to go back across the street. We only have an hour left to get ready for dinner. We'll see you tomorrow." Grant took Kelli's arm and led her to the front door. "Show time."

Stepping out of the bakery, Kelli did a good job of looking nervous because she was. She and Grant paused at the edge of the sidewalk to scan the street. The late afternoon sun made looking to the west difficult, so Kelli was glad when they entered the café. They were surprised when they saw a police officer in the back near Tracy's office.

The officer stood, and even though there were no diners nearby, he quietly said, "Miss Mills, I have checked the basement and back entrance. It's safe."

"Thank you. I really appreciate that," Kelli replied softly. "Tracy keeps the main back entrance locked. We will keep the apartment's back door locked." The officer nodded and left through the café's front door.

Without saying a word, Grant took Kelli's hand and led her through the back of the restaurant, up the stairs and into his apartment. He placed a finger over his mouth for her to not speak. After turning the television on to the news station, he placed both radios next to it.

Walking into the kitchen, he smiled and said, "If anyone

is listening, they will get all the latest news."

Kelli grinned. "Well, we need for them to be informed, don't we?"

Grant smiled and winked.

"Do you want to change?" he asked. "I think we have enough time to to do that before we have to be downstairs for dinner."

"Yes," Kelli said. "I want out of these shoes. Not my favorites."

A few minutes later, Kelli came out of her bedroom. Grant had changed into jeans, a three button knit shirt and athletic shoes. She smiled. She loved the way he looked in jeans.

Grant looked up to see Kelli wearing a light green sundress. It had a low neckline, and the back was only straps crossing to the waistline. The slim skirt hugged her hips.

"Are you sure you want to wear that?" Grant asked, frowning.

Kelli placed a white jersey sweater over the dress.

"Yes. I'll take the sweater off when we go outside. I intend to lure this creep out of the mud and into the open."

Grant walked over to Kelli and kissed her.

"Would you rather we stay here?" he asked.

"No," she answered. "We need to do as Chief Sanders said."

"I know," Grant said. He looked at his watch, "It's almost six. We'd better go." Grant led Kelli down the stairs and into the café. They found a booth, ordered, and ate dinner.

After they finished, Grant led Kelli outside to the sidewalk on Main Street.

"I guess this is the next part of the show," Kelli said and took off her sweater, handing it to Grant. "Would you mind carrying this?" she asked sweetly. "It's quite warm out here."

"Sure," Grant said, smiling as he took the sweater. "Although with that dress, I should ask you to keep it on. You are a vision."

Kelli looked up at Grant and smiled. The sun was getting low in the sky, softening the shadows, and complimenting Kelli's complexion. Her long blond hair softly brushed her back and shoulders.

"Why Mr. Sparks. I believe you just gave me a compliment." She laughed and took his arm.

Grant and Kelli slowly walked to the bookstore. They were walking east, and the park was behind them. Knowing Aaron liked hiding in the park, Grant traced his index finger along the straps that criss-crossed Kelli's back.

Kelli leaned her head against Grant's shoulder. "I think I wish this wasn't an act. I like the way that feels."

"Me, too," Grant whispered.

The bookstore was closed, of course, but they stood looking into the windows at the display. Kelli turned in front of the window, pulled the hair off her back and fanned her neck. She hoped she was giving Aaron a view of her bare back. They stood there talking. Kelli turned around and faced the street. Grant followed her lead and turned too.

She turned her face to the setting sun, smiled, and turned around with her arms outstretched.

"I love this time of year," she said. Kelli stretched her arms up as if embracing the waning light. "I hate that the days are getting shorter. It will soon be winter."

Grant watched her. She was acting as if they were on a date and there was no danger. She was acting as if she were trying to get his attention. Well, she had it. He smiled, took her hand and turned her back to the café.

He whispered in her ear, "Good show. Now look surprised, look around, and start to act nervous like you forgot all about Aaron for a while."

Kelli gasped, placed a hand over her mouth and looked around. She grabbed Grant's arm and moved closer like she wanted his protection. Grant put his arm around her shoulders, and they headed back toward the café. He didn't have to wonder if he looked protective of Kelli, because that was just how he was feeling. He would do anything to keep her safe.

Kelli slowed their walk. She loved the feel of Grant's arm around her. Aaron or no Aaron, she wanted to prolong the sensation. Finally, at the door of the café, Kelli took her sweater from Grant and put it back on before entering the building. The show was over.

Aaron watched Grant and Kelli walk down the street. He was seething with anger. Grant was walking with his girl. Kelli looked beautiful in the green sundress, but he was angry with her. She should not be wearing that revealing of a dress for anyone but him. She would have to be punished. Aaron smiled. Her punishment would be watching him hurt Grant, then she would be willing to do whatever he said to keep her lover from suffering.

"Damn," the plainclothes officer said. "That woman knows how to put on a show. If that doesn't bring the creep out of the woodwork, I don't know what will. She's beautiful."

"Tell it," the other, older officer said while watching the street. "Something tells me that Blalock is watching. I just can't figure out where he is."

A flash of light in the park caught the first officer's eye. He looked that way. He could see a man with binoculars watching the street.

"There he is," he said nodding toward the park. He's crouched in some shadows and bushes. I wouldn't have seen him if I hadn't seen the reflection off his binoculars.

"Good," the older officer said and reported the sighting. "We know where he is and where he's watching from. The park must be where he's staying most of the time. I hate that. Children play in there."

When Kelli and Grant disappeared back into the café, the senior officer said, "Let's stroll down by the park. Maybe we can catch a glimpse of him and maybe even arrest him." The two officers walked by where they had seen Aaron, but he had already gone.

"I'll let the Chief know what we saw. Let's hope he's here in the morning," the senior officer said softly.

Grant and Kelli walked through the café to the back, climbed the stairs and went into the apartment. They entered and Grant locked the door behind them. Kelli took her shoes off and walked into the kitchen. Grant walked around the island and met her on the other side.

He put his arms around her and kissed her, then led her to the couch.

"Let's sit," he said. "I felt like Aaron was watching us the whole time we were on Main Street. I feel the need to just hold you and make sure you're safe."

"I know what you mean," Kelli said. "Part of me enjoyed the evening with you, but part of me just felt creepy, almost violated from knowing he was watching."

Grant pulled Kelli into his arms.

"You're safe," he reassured her. Kelli smiled and closed her eyes, enjoying the sensation of being in Grant's arms.

After a few moments of silence, Grant said, "This feels like it's going to be over in a day or two. Will you be glad to be back to normal?"

"Yes," Kelli said, smiling, "but I may not want to leave here. You may have to put up with me for the rest of your life."

"I can live with that," he said smiling.

CHAPTER 23

Kelli was sleeping deeply when her alarm sounded. She wiped the grogginess from her eyes, turned the sound off and got out of bed.

Grant woke to his alarm. His phone read six am. He groaned and rolled back under the covers. He was tired, but it was time to get up and get ready. Then he smiled, thinking of Kelli. Never had he ever felt this way for a woman. He knew where these feelings were heading, and he was fine with that. The journey of falling in love with Kelli Mills would be a roller coaster of passion, friendship, and the occasional argument thrown in.

Unfortunately, he couldn't be completely sure about how Kelli felt until this nightmare with Aaron was over. His biggest fear was that Kelli would transfer some of her disgust of Aaron to him. They were cousins. They were nothing alike, but still, that familial connection was there. He had never hated anyone in his life, but he was getting very close to hating Aaron. If his cousin completely ruined any chance he had with Kelli, he's not sure he would ever be able to forgive Aaron.

The only thing he could do was make Kelli fall in love

with him, but that would have to wait. Now it was time to get dressed and get this morning run over.

Grant found Kelli already dressed in running attire and sitting at the kitchen island staring out at the street.

"Are you okay?" he asked.

"I need coffee," she answered. "You know that, but unfortunately, the coffee maker won't recognize that and go any faster."

Grant laughed. "Do you want anything to eat before we go to the park?"

"No," she answered. "I'll just drink a cup of coffee and some water. I'm too nervous to eat."

"I know. Me, too," Grant said as he watched hot coffee slowly drip into the carafe. Finally, it was finished, and he filled two mugs with coffee. He passed one to Kelli. The two sat in companionable silence as they sipped the hot liquid and listened to the traffic on Main Street.

When Kelli finished her coffee, she stood.

Grant looked at her running clothes, "You are too sexy to be in public. Do you know that? You'll not only get Aaron's attention, but every other red blooded male running in the park this morning."

Kelli smiled. "Well, I'm glad you think so." She had on tight spandex shorts, a low-cut sports bra that criss-crossed in the back, and a loose-fitting tank top.

"Let's hope Aaron is there and thinks so, too," she said. "Maybe he will make a move and the police can arrest him. I'm ready to get on with my life. Is there an easy way to get to the park from your back entrance? I'm not comfortable going through the café wearing these particular jogging clothes. They're not exactly appropriate for dining."

"We can go the long way around," Grant said. He looked at his watch. They had ten minutes. Going to the television, he picked up the radios.

He put the device in his ear and asked, "Is anyone monitoring this radio yet?"

"Yes," an officer said. "We just turned it on to test the frequencies. Thanks for trying it out."

"We're going to go out the back door and around to the front. We just wanted to let you know," Grant informed him.

"Thanks for the info. We have people back there. It makes sense that you would do that. What is your route to the park?" he asked.

"We will go around the building to Oak Street then to Main Street," Grant said. "We'll cross Main Street and go into the park. We will start running at the park entrance."

"OK. Does Kelli have her radio in?" he asked.

"Not yet. Do you need to talk with her?" Grant asked.

"No. Just tell her to let us know when she's wearing it. We just want to know," he said.

"Okay. We're getting ready to leave," Grant said. He handed Kelli her radio.

"Let the officer know when you have it in your ear," he told her.

Kelli placed the radio in her ear and said, "I have the radio in place."

"We can hear you. Can you hear us?" the officer asked.

"Yes," she answered.

"Okay. Go on to the park," the officer instructed. "We will monitor you. If you hear us on the radio don't stop to listen. Act as if nothing has changed in your run."

"Okay," Kelli and Grant said together. Grant locked the

apartment door behind them and placed the key in a zippered pocket of his shorts. He placed his cell phone in another pocket.

"I'm glad you have the phone," Kelli said grinning. "I don't have a place to carry one."

"No kidding!" exclaimed Grant. "You're going to attract some serious attention in that running outfit."

"That's the plan," Kelli said. "I want to bring that scum out of the ooze."

Grant held Kelli's hand as they walked around the building to Oak Street. The tree lined street had red maple leaves starting to fall onto the sidewalk. They stopped at Main Street before crossing to the park. The street was busy with school buses and parents taking their children to school.

Finding a break in the traffic, Kelli and Grant crossed the street to the park. The two stopped, stretched for a few minutes then began to slowly jog.

"That's good," they heard. "Keep a nice steady pace."

Kelli and Grant jogged beside each other. After a few minutes, Grant noticed Kelli holding her side.

"Let's walk," he said. Kelli nodded in agreement.

"You're in better shape than I am," she said. "It didn't take long to get a cramp in my side."

"Walk it off," they heard in their ears. "No need to run the whole way. The longer you're in the park, the better chance we have of spotting Blalock. Take the path on the right when you get to the small intersection. It's less traveled."

Grant pointed to the right path and Kelli followed him. They made it look like a spontaneous decision. There were very few people on this path which made Kelli slightly nervous. Grant noticed.

"Are you all right?" he asked her.

"It just feels deserted," Kelli said. "It's a little unnerving. Let's jog and get through here quickly." Grant picked up their pace.

Grant and Kelli heard a rush of background conversations on the radio. Aaron had been spotted in the park, but he wasn't on the jogging paths. Multiple voices called out commands and responses.

Grant saw a jogger coming toward them. The man stopped.

"Do you know what's going on in the park?" he asked, gesturing behind him. "There are a lot of people around the picnic area. Are they planning something?"

Grant and Kelli stopped.

Grant shrugged, "No idea. I didn't realize there was anyone else here. This path has been pretty deserted."

"Yeah, well, I was just curious," the man said smiling.

Grant and Kelli watched as the man jogged down the path away from them.

"Good save," they heard on the radio. "Take the next right on the path and you will come out at the front of the park on Main Street. Just sit on a bench and talk."

Grant and Kelli did as they were instructed.

After sitting on the bench, Kelli said, "Well, that was a unique experience."

Grant chuckled. "I guess you could call it that. Do you have any appointments today?"

"No. But I need to work downstairs again," Kelli answered then asked, "Do we need to take the radios to work?"

"No," the man answered. "Go ahead back to the apartment and finish your day. Blalock was spotted in the park but by the time officers were in place, he had disappeared. We'll do this same procedure tomorrow. Go about your normal day. Be assured that there are officers watching for him constantly."

Grant said to Kelli, "OK. Let's go back and change for work." He took her hand, helped her up from the bench, and they walked back to the apartment.

Aaron was out of breath when he got into his car. That was the closest he had ever come to being caught. All he had been seeing were uniformed policemen. There were plainsclothes cops in the park, had to be. There had been too many men chasing him. Well, they made a mistake, because now he knew who to look for.

Aaron was driving safely, but he was furious. Kelli had looked way to sexy to be jogging with Grant. Aaron drove several miles down the interstate until he thought it was safe to stop for food. The more he thought about Kelli, the angrier he got. Kelli would have already been his if it hadn't been for his irritating cousin. It was time he dealt with Grant.

A sausage biscuit and coffee helped calm Aaron enough he could think more clearly. He smiled. A plan had just come to his mind. Why hadn't he thought about this before. Kelli was going to get rid of Grant for him.

CHAPTER 24

Grant stopped and locked the door to the apartment after they returned from the park. Kelli walked down the hall to her bedroom. She gathered her clothes and walked across the hall to her bathroom.

Kelli turned on the water and got into the shower. She closed her eyes and let the hot water flow over her body, soothing her tense muscles. Kelli soaped up and rinsed off twice. She felt like she would never feel clean again. In ten minutes, Kelli was dressed and ready to go out the door. Instead of drying her hair all the way, she had used hair gel and scrunched it so it would dry curled.

Grant looked at her and said, "That's a new look. It's nice. Do you do that often?"

"Only when I'm short on time. The hair isn't dry; it's just full of gel," she explained.

"I'm not even going to try to understand. Are you ready to go?" he asked.

Kelli picked up her computer bag and purse. "Lead on, oh computer genius."

"Don't you ever forget that either," Grant said grinning.

"Oh, brother," Kelli moaned. "There's no shrinking that

head today, is there."

Grant laughed and locked the door behind them.

Candy watched Grant and Kelli cross the street and enter the bakery. They walked in and ordered muffins and coffee.

"Well," she asked. "How did the jog in the park go?"

Kelli looked around and saw two women at the cash register.

"Uneventful," Kelli said quietly. "All I got out of that stress was the need to use hair gel because I ran out of time to dry my hair."

"Shoot. I was hoping they would get him," Candy whispered.

"I think he may have been spotted," Grant said after the women left the bakery. "We heard a lot of commotion on the radios, but nothing was resolved. I guess we wait until we hear from one of the police officers."

"We'll be in the basement," Kelli told Candy as they took their muffins and coffee. "I still have a lot to do there." She held up the phone. "Call me if you need me."

Candy watched them get on the elevator. She sighed in frustration. If this was not resolved soon, it was going to interfere with the events they had scheduled for the weekend. Plus, every day Aaron avoided arrest was another day he could harm Kelli.

Grant and Kelli sat at the table eating their muffins and setting up their computers. Kelli's phone rang.

"Cotton Catering and Events." Kelli's face paled. She looked at Grant and put the phone on speaker.

"Hello, Kelli," Aaron said. Grant got his phone and started recording the conversation. He picked up Kelli's cell phone and called the police to let them know Aaron was on the company phone line.

"Aaron," she said, trying to keep her voice calm. "What can I do for you?"

"I saw you last night," Aaron said. His voice was calm and low. Kelli thought it was like the calm before a storm. You knew something was coming, but you didn't know what to expect.

"You were walking with Grant," Aaron continued, "and you were wearing the dress of a slut. You know better than to wear dresses that are so tight they show your muscles when you walk or that are low in the front and have no back, except for a few straps."

Kelli felt a chill run up her spine. He had been watching her very closely last night. Kelli's knuckles turned white as she gripped the table.

"Do you know how angry that makes me, Kelli? I saw him rub your back. You know you should not allow that, Kelli. Grant should know better, too. I'm going to have to have a little chat with him about that. Maybe a little physical chat," Aaron said calmly with a hint of a smile. "Maybe I'll let you watch that, Kelli. That should teach you not to cross me."

Kelli was glad she was still sitting when she started trembling. Her biggest fear that Aaron would try to hurt Grant was coming true.

"Did you sleep with him, Kelli?" Aaron asked calmly. The question caught Kelli completely off guard. She wasn't expecting him to jump that far ahead with his delusions.

"I think you did," Aaron continued. "Now I really need to punish you, and I need to punish Grant, too. He has betrayed family. I think my first punishment for you will be to watch me punish Grant. I saw you running with him this morning, too. I saw you wearing those tight running shorts. How could you go out in public looking like that?"

Aaron paused, and the line was quiet. Kelli could tell he was still on the line because she heard him drumming his fingers on a hard surface. Then Kelli realized that was the only sound she heard. There were no background noises to give any indication as to where he might be hiding. Kelli jumped when Aaron spoke again.

"Kelli, I will forgive all this if you just come away with me," Aaron said. His voice had changed, and Kelli thought it sounded like he had been thinking and decided on a plan.

"We can be together and forget any of this ever happened. I won't punish Grant, and you can forget you ever met him." Aaron paused then said, "I'm waiting for an answer."

"Aaron," Kelli said, fighting to keep her voice calm and level. "I have told you over and over, I'm not going out with you. I have a relationship with Grant, and I will not betray that." Kelli cringed at the expletives and filth that spewed from Aaron's mouth.

Kelli looked at Grant, who was standing at the basement door, and mouthed, "Can I just hang up on him?"

Grant shook his head no and gestured with his hand to keep talking.

He mouthed, "Police are trying to tell where he is calling from. Keep him on the line."

Kelli nodded in understanding.

"Kelli, do you hear me? Are you still there?" Aaron demanded.

"I'm here," Kelli answered timidly. "Why are you being

so mean, Aaron. I haven't done anything to you but be honest. I have no feelings for you. My feelings are for Grant. Can you not honor that?"

The phone's speaker crackled as Aaron sighed loudly.

"Kelli, you are lying to yourself and to me. You belong to me, Kelli, and I will not let anyone come between us. Not even Grant. I know Grant has persuaded you to be with him and that he is influencing your decisions against me. Don't worry about that. I can get rid of Grant so we can be together."

Aaron paused, and Kelli did not answer.

"Kelli," Aaron said, his words sounding clipped, "I'm running out of patience. If you don't want Grant punished, then you need to come to me. Kelli, I'm willing to kill Grant if I need to."

"Aaron, no," Kelli said crying. "You can't be serious. Why would you hurt Grant? Even if I weren't in a relationship with Grant, I wouldn't be in one with you. Can't you understand that?"

Kelli's blood ran cold when she heard the dark, flat voice say, "I'm tired of waiting. This is my last warning, Kelli. Come to me or Grant dies. It's that simple."

"Where are you?" she asked.

"I'm not going to tell you. If you're serious, go to the park tonight," he said.

"No, Aaron. If I come, it will be in the daylight. Do not expect me after dark," she said.

"Come tonight or Grant will be dead by the morning," he threatened.

"All right, Aaron. Just don't hurt Grant. Please don't hurt Grant. He's no match for you," Kelli said in a pleading voice.

Grant saw Kelli's demeanor change. He was sure she had a plan.

"Please, Aaron. You know Grant could never overcome you. You could kill him with one fist to the face and you know it," Kelli said.

There was silence on the phone for a few seconds.

"I'm glad you can recognize who the better man is, Kelli," Aaron said calmly. "Since you have pled so graciously for Grant's life, I may consider letting him live, but only if you meet me in the park tonight at sunset."

"All right, Aaron. You win," Kelli said.

"Bring a packed suitcase. You won't be back for a while," Aaron said.

"Aaron, I have a job, and I'm in charge of events this weekend. I can't leave town right now," Kelli said. "I will meet you, but I can't go anywhere with you yet. I want to keep my job. We can only talk tonight. I know you understand how important my job will be to us. We will need money if we're going to be together. We can talk and make plans. No one needs to know we are there. It will be just us."

"You have to leave Grant's apartment, Kelli," Aaron said. "I can't have you staying at another man's place." Aaron hesitated. "Did you call the police, Kelli?"

"No. Why, Aaron?" she asked. "Why would the police want you?"

"Tonight, at sunset, Kelli, or Grant dies."

Before Aaron could end the call Kelli quickly said, "Wait, Aaron. How will I find you?"

"I'll find you," Aaron said abruptly and ended the call.

Kelli's hand shook as she picked up the phone to make sure the call was disconnected. Grant was still on her phone talking with the police. She wanted to scream in frustration, and she wanted to cry with fear. She was going to have to go to the park tonight; she knew it. The police would ask her to go, and Grant would ask her not to go.

Kelli sat and stared at the phone. She heard Grant end the call with the police and waited for the reaction that she knew was coming.

"You can't go to the park, Kelli. He can't be trusted," Grant said as he walked across the room and sat down beside her.

"I have to, Grant. It's the only way to end this. The police will have the place surrounded. It will be okay," Kelli said. She sat staring into space. Grant wondered what she was thinking.

Kellie stood. "I need to talk to Candy."

Kelli took her purse and climbed the stairs to the first floor. She found Candy in the kitchen.

Candy looked up to see Kelli walking toward her. The look on Kelli's face was a mixture of anxiety, anger, and determination.

"Kelli. Is everything okay?" Candy asked.

"Aaron just called," Kelli said. "I have to meet him in the park tonight. Grant was on the phone with the police, so I expect them here any moment. But I have a favor to ask."

"Sure. What do you need?" Candy asked.

Kelli reached into her purse, extracted twenty dollars and handed it to Candy.

"Will you go to the hardware store and buy a pepper spray," Kelli asked. "I don't want the police to know I have it. I will meet Aaron, but I won't go empty handed."

"Put your money away," Candy said. "I've got this." Candy got her purse and walked out to the front of the bakery.

"Will you watch the place for a minute?," Candy asked Ellen as she walked past the cash register. "I need to go to the hardware store." Ellen said she would, and Candy left the building.

About ten minutes later Candy came back into the store with a small bag in her hand. She took it to the back of the kitchen where she handed it to Kelli. Kelli pulled out the spray and read the directions. When she was confident that she knew how to use it, Kelli put it in her purse.

"Thanks," she said to Candy.

Candy watched Kelli purchase two servings of quiche and two glasses of tea and take them to the basement. Kelli was on a mission, and that mission was to get Aaron Blalock.

Kelli entered the basement with the food and tea. Grant was on her phone with the police department. She held the food up to make sure he knew it was there then placed it on the table. Kelli took the next chair and sat down to eat her lunch. Eventually Grant ended his call.

"I take it there is a plan?" Kelli asked.

"Yes," Grant said. "The only problem is that you can't wear your earpiece to meet Aaron. They're afraid he will see it and react badly."

"I think they're right about that," Kelli said.

"But they want to place a tracking device on you just on the chance they lose you in the dark," Grant said. "I don't even want to think about that possibility."

Kelli looked at Grant. She could see the stress in his face.

"What do they want you to do during all of this?" she asked.

"You are to leave through the café and cross the street just as the sun is setting," Grant said, sounding sadly resigned. "Sit on the second bench from the entrance. Officers will be all over the park and Main Street. After you have been sitting for a few minutes, I am to come out of the café like I'm looking for you. You are to act like you are hiding from me. They're hoping that scenario will make Aaron overconfident and reveal himself."

"I don't like this, Kelli," Grant said firmly. "I don't like the idea of you being alone in the park with Aaron, even if there is a multitude of law enforcement in the vicinity."

Kelli got up, walked over to Grant, put her arms around him and rested her head on his chest.

"I know," she said. "I'm not crazy about it either, but it's the only way I can think of to end this. I'm tired of being scared. I'm tired of having my life turned upside down because of a delusional idiot. I'm just tired of it all, and I want it finished."

Grant wrapped his arms around Kelli and rested his cheek on the top of her head.

"He's crazy, Kelli," Grant stressed. "He's delusional, and I think he's psychotic. There's no way to predict what he will do. That's what worries me. He is slippery and unpredictable."

Kelli pulled away and said, "Eat your lunch. I have a few more things to do, then we can go back across the street."

Grant sat at his computer and tried to work while Kelli finished her task.

"When you first started working," he said, "I was so

distracted that I thought I couldn't work, but this is worse. There's no way I can work. All I can do is worry about tonight." He closed his computer. "Are you about finished?"

Kelli stopped and said, "I'm all done. Let's go tell Candy we're leaving. We have things to do to get ready for a police stakeout."

When they reached the bakery door, Kelli said, "Let's act like we've had an argument. If Aaron is watching, he will take that as a sign that he's winning."

Kelli and Grant walked out onto the sidewalk. Grant took her arm. Kelli jerked away from his hand and started across the street alone with her arms folded and head down. Grant waited a moment, acted frustrated, then followed her.

Aaron watched Kelli and Grant cross the street to the café. When he saw Kelli jerk her arm away from Grant and walk ahead, he smiled. He was winning.

CHAPTER 25

Kelli was feeling tired and overwhelmed. As soon as Grant finished locking the apartment's door, he watched her walk toward him. The room was dim because the lights were off and the curtains were closed, but he could see the fatigue and worry on Kelli's face. He held out his arms. She walked into his embrace.

Kelli wrapped her arms around Grant and leaned her cheek against his shoulder.

"I didn't like pretending to be mad at you," she said. "I had enough of that when I first started to work."

"All we did was argue," Grant said, smiling with the memory. "It's a wonder Paul and Candy kept us employed. I like being friends much better."

"Just friends?" Kelli asked.

"No. We can never be just friends," Grant said, tightening the embrace. "I'm falling in love with you, Kelli. You can never be just my friend."

Kelli felt the warmth of Grant's words against her temple. The sensation made her feel secure.

"I know. I feel the same," Kelli said, moving her hands along Grant's back. "I don't think I could stand not having you in my life."

Grant kissed her. "Please say you won't leave me. I don't think I could survive." He kissed her again and held her tight, feeling the danger of the evening looming ahead of them.

Kelli and Grant continued the embrace for a few more minutes. When the shadows in the room began to lengthen, Kelli broke the embrace and sighed. It was time to get ready.

After showering, Kelli fixed her hair, and put on her makeup. When she started to put on lipstick, Kelli's hand was shaking so badly she opted for chapstick.

Kelli chose to wear a summer dress with a full skirt that had deep pockets in the seam. Instead of sandals, she wore lightweight athletic shoes. While Grant was still in his room, she placed the can of pepper spray in her right pocket. Turning and twirling in front of the mirror, Kelli was glad the full skirt completely hid the small can.

Grant walked down the hall and saw Kelli standing in the kitchen drinking from a water bottle, her hands had a slight tremor. He had on jeans and a T-shirt. Their plan was to have dinner on the balcony and stage another fight. He sat on a stool and drew her into his arms.

"I don't want you to do this," Grant whispered. "You know that, right?"

"Yes. The truth is, I don't want to do this either," Kelli told him. "But I see no other way out. My reassurance is that there are probably a dozen unseen law enforcement personnel surrounding the park. I hope they apprehend him before he gets to me." She stood and picked up the two plates of food. "You can bring the drinks and silverware."

Grant followed Kelli to the balcony. The sun was already starting to get low in the sky. They sat at the table eating. Kelli looked sullen and petulant. Grant looked tired and exasperated. Kelli ate just enough to keep her stomach from growling and feeling empty. Any more food, and she felt like she would throw it all up.

The sun was setting. Grant leaned toward Kelli and pointed his fork toward her.

He gestured and said firmly, "We can start the argument. I say we call it off."

Kelli stood and said loudly, "I said no!" She turned and stormed off the balcony.

Grant noticed people stop walking on the street and look up at the balcony. Kelli had been very persuasive. He remained looking angry and unwilling to go after her. He heard the apartment door slam. A few minutes later, he saw her exit the café and walk to the park.

Grant stood. He pretended to be angry, threw his napkin on the table and stormed into the apartment. Grant quickly closed and locked the balcony doors. He ran across the apartment and picked up his ear radio. Taking time to lock his door behind him, Grant ran down the stairs, placing the radio in his ear. After casually walking through the café, he opened the door and walked out to the sidewalk. He looked up and down the street as if looking for Kelli.

"Walk up and down the street," the voice on his radio said. "Kelli is sitting on the bench." Grant did as he was instructed.

"Now cross the street to the park," the officer said into the radio. "Keep looking up and down the sidewalk before entering the park. Remember, you don't know where she went."

Grant crossed Main Street and went to the park entrance. He started to enter when he was almost knocked to the side by a woman who was power walking.

Grant quickly avoided the women and said, "Excuse me. I didn't see you." The woman ignored him, keeping her face turned away from him, and never broke her stride.

Before Grant started looking for Kelli again, the woman caught his attention. She had a very masculine build and stride. Her athletic shoes were obviously men's shoes and were caked with mud.

Grant stood still then turned around and quietly said, "I think Aaron is dressed as the woman walking into the park. He couldn't resist bumping me. I wouldn't have noticed him if he hadn't done that."

"Good work. We saw the woman but didn't realize it was Blalock," the voice said.

Kelli walked quickly across the street, found the bench she was supposed to use in the park and sat down. Her heart pounded in her ears. It seemed like the minutes were dragging into hours. She kept looking around. A large woman power walked past her on the trail, but Kelli ignored her and kept watching for Aaron.

Aaron liked his disguise. A cheap purchase from a thrift store, and he looked like a woman trying to lose weight. He started his power walk when he saw Kelli walk across the street. Aaron smiled. He came into the park entrance and Grant was there looking for Kelli. He walked so close that Grant had to jump to the side. Grant really was the weaker cousin, Aaron thought. He was too stupid to realize who Aaron was.

Kelli was on the bench when he walked by. She didn't recognize him. Good, he thought. Surprise was on his side. He left the trail and circled back behind Kelli's bench. Aaron stood for a moment and watched her. Kelli kept looking back and forth. He smiled; she was looking for him. This was a good sign. Grant has already lost. Aaron quietly walked up behind her.

"Hello, Kelli. You came," he said.

Kelli was startled by the voice behind her and jumped up. She turned around and saw the woman. Confused, she was trying to reconcile the man's voice with the woman standing in front of her. Even though he was standing in the evening shadows, Kelli recognized his face.

"Aaron?" she asked incredulously.

"Yes," he said with an arrogant smile. "I have many disguises. I play many roles. Tonight, I played the role of the woman." He laughed. "They saw the real me on the other side of the park. All the plainclothes policemen are over there. They don't know I put on this disguise."

Kelli felt her stomach drop with a sudden fear that she may be on her own.

Aaron took off the wig and kerchief. "Now, I play the role of the victor."

Kelli stood and backed away, careful to keep the bench between her and the man.

"What do you mean by victor?" she asked.

"I won," he answered with a smile. "I have you and Grant doesn't. In fact, I walked past Grant just a few minutes ago, and he had no clue it was me." Aaron slowly walked around the bench as he spoke.

"Of course," Kelli said, keeping her voice calm as she carefully put her right hand in her skirt pocket. "Grant couldn't win against you. We both knew that."

"You can come with me, now," Aaron said, "but we need to get going. There are probably people still looking for me."

"I can't," Kelli said. "I told you, I need to work, but you haven't been listening. We can make another plan."

Aaron flushed with anger.

"And I told you, we're leaving together. Don't make me mad so that I have to punish you, Kelli." He started to walk around the bench.

Kelli moved to the other side, keeping the bench between them.

"What are you doing?" he asked.

"We need to talk, Aaron," Kelli said. "I can't go with you tonight. You aren't listening to me."

Aaron grew uncontrollably angry. He snarled, jumped onto the bench seat and launched himself over the bench toward Kelli.

Kelli was surprised and started to run, but Aaron grabbed her arm. He pulled her to him.

"I told you, I win. You're mine. We leave together tonight," Aaron said and moved his head to kiss her. "We will have all the time in the world together."

Kelli felt bile rise in her throat. She pursed her lips and pulled away from Aaron. She tried to get the pepper spray container out of her pocket but it got caught in the folds of the skirt.

Kelli turned and ran from Aaron. Aaron ran after her. He reached for her arm, but Kelli dodged his hand. Aaron missed her arm but clutched a handful of fabric from her dress.

Kelli heard fabric rip and felt herself falling backward toward Aaron. He caught her, and Kelli started to scream. Aaron put his hand over her mouth, lost his balance, and the two fell to the ground.

Kelli grabbed a handful of dirt and threw it into Aaron's face. Aaron's anger became uncontrollable. He reached up to hit Kelli in the face, but Kelli had managed to get the pepper spray from her pocket. She aimed it at Aaron and pressed the trigger. The irritating liquid coated Aaron's face.

Aaron's hand stopped in mid air. He clawed at his face and screamed.

"Aahh!" he screamed as his hands flew to his face. "What did you do?"

Grant had been told by the police to stay at the park entrance, but when he heard the commotion, he disobeyed the orders and ran into the park where he knew Kelli was supposed to be.

The police officers who had fallen for Aaron's distraction were still on the other side of the park. They began running toward the bench.

Grant reached the bench, but no one was there. He heard Aaron screaming a few yards away and saw Kelli standing over him. Aaron was writhing on the ground holding his face. Every time he tried to get up in Kelli's direction, she sprayed his face again.

"Stop!" he yelled. "My eyes!"

Three police officers rolled Aaron onto his stomach and cuffed his hands behind his back. It took all three to get him to his feet. He was screaming that he had been blinded by his girlfriend who was supposed to be leaving with him. He wanted to press charges.

Grant slowly approached Kelli. She stood tense, alert and ready to spray the man again. The look of determination on her face told him she was not going to let Aaron win.

"It's over, Kelli," Grant said calmly. She looked at him and blinked. He could tell she was having difficulty realizing she was safe. Grant ran his hand along her arm and gently took the pepper spray.

"You did good, Kelli," he said, taking her in his arms. "I'm so proud of you."

Kelli let Grant wrap her in his arms. She sighed with relief. It was finally over.

"I hope I blinded the creep," she mumbled into his chest.

Grant chuckled. "I feel good knowing he will always remember being taken down by a woman."

"I like that," Kelli said with a faint smile. "Poetic justice at its best."

Chief Sanders came over to talk with Kelli and Grant. He thanked them for their cooperation, and he praised Kelli for her planning and quick thinking. He asked them both to come to the police department the next day to make a statement for the final report, but they could leave for now.

Chapter 26

B lue lights flashed and reflected off the brick facade of the surrounding buildings. Police cars from three cities blocked all the entrances to the park, and a crowd had formed on Main Street to watch what was happening.

Kelli and Grant stood back as a police officer escorted Aaron in handcuffs to one of the cars. Aaron looked over and locked eyes with Grant then Kelli. It was a look of pure hatred. Aaron's eyes never left them as the car drove away. Only after it turned onto a side street did Aaron look ahead.

When they stepped back into the apartment Grant asked Kelli, "Are you okay? You had a close encounter with a mad man."

"Oddly enough, I'm fine," Kelli said. "I was prepared with a can of pepper spray. I knew the police were nearby, and I knew you were somewhere in the park. While I knew there was the possibility that he could get violent, I didn't think he would. I thought he was too busy wanting to win against you to hurt me at that moment."

The memory of the moment she knew she could be in

danger came back to haunt Kelli like a bolt of lightening. She shook her head, telling herself again that it was over.

Kelli's cell phone rang. It was Candy.

"Hello," she answered.

"Are you all right?" Candy asked. "I was closing the bakery when I saw the blue lights and a lot of policemen. I assumed it had something to do with you."

"Yes. It's over, thank goodness. I'll tell you all about it tomorrow. It's quite a story," Kelli told her. "I'll be in tomorrow morning. I will just have to go to the police department at some point to make a statement."

"Do whatever you need to do, Kelli," Candy said. "Let's get this wrapped up and behind us."

"Thank you, Candy," Kelli said. "Thank you for your support and understanding through all this."

"That's what friends do. I'll see you tomorrow," Candy said and ended the call.

Kelli turned to Grant. He was alarmed at the dark circles under her eyes.

"Are you all right?" he asked. "Do you need anything? Food?"

"No," Kelli replied. "I feel like a huge weight has been lifted, but I'm suddenly very tired. I just want to go to bed."

Grant nodded and watched Kelli disappear into her room. He knew how she felt. The events of the last few days had taken a toll on his energy, too. He made sure the doors were locked then walked down the hall to his room to sleep.

Lying in bed, Grant relived the events of the last several days, especially those of that evening. He will never forget the terror he felt when he realized that Aaron had gotten to Kelli before he could. He will never forget the look of hatred Aaron had given him as the car drove away or the feeling of relief he felt at that same moment. Just before falling asleep, Grant admitted to himself that he was in love with Kelli. He fell asleep smiling.

Kelli woke to the smell of coffee. She looked at the clock; it was seven. Smiling, she took a shower, dried her hair, got dressed and walked out to join Grant in the kitchen.

Grant looked up when he saw Kelli coming down the hall.

"You look rested. Did you sleep well?" he asked, smiling.

"Like a baby, but I still need coffee," she said taking a cup from the cabinet. Kelli poured herself a cup of coffee, picked up a plate then cut a portion from the cheese Danish on the island.

She took a bite and smiled, "This one is from Candy's."

"It's easy to tell, isn't it?" Grant said. "She's so talented."

Kelli nodded. "Her talent makes my job easy." Kelli looked at her phone. "Time to go to work. Are you going over now or later?"

"I'll go now," Grant said. "I have the on-call tonight, but I also have some work to catch up on because I didn't work my full hours yesterday or the day before."

Kelli and Grant spent the first hour of their workday sitting in the bakery retelling the events of the evening before to Candy and Paul. Then Grant went to his office. Kelli checked her calendar and prepared for a client's appointment that afternoon.

At ten o'clock, Kelli's cell phone rang. She didn't recognize the number. For a sudden, very slight moment, Kelli relived the anxiety she had been having whenever she saw an unknown number on her phone. She wondered how long it would be before that would stop happening.

"Hello," she said.

"Kelli, this is Chief Sanders." Kelli felt herself relax when she realized it wasn't Aaron. "Can you come to the department? There are some questions that we have about this case that maybe you can answer."

"I can do that. Do you want me to bring Grant?" she asked. "Also, I have an appointment at three o'clock. Do I need to reschedule that?"

"Yes. Please bring Grant, too, but I don't think you need to reschedule your afternoon. When you get here, just ask for me at the desk," he said and ended the call.

Kelli walked out of her office and into the hallway. She knocked on Grant's door.

"Come in," she heard.

Kelli opened the door. Grant looked up from his computer and smiled.

"Hey. What's up?"

"Chief Sanders called," Kelli said. "He wants us to come to the department to answer some questions."

*****

Kelli's car was still behind the bakery where it had been for the past four days. She drove across town to the police department. They went in the front door and at the main desk, they asked for Chief Sanders. Within a few minutes he came to the front and escorted them to a conference room on the side of the building.

"Have a seat," he said. "I'll get the others."

When he left the room, Kelli looked at Grant, "Others?

What does that mean?"

"I imagine the representatives from the other cities are still here," Grant said.

The door opened and Chief Sanders returned with six other men. They all took seats at the table.

Chief Sanders looked at Kelli and Grant and said, "I know the two of you are ready for this is over, but we have some questions. Kelli, where did you first meet Aaron Blalock?"

"I was working at a wedding reception on the second floor of the bakery," Kelli told him. "Cotton Catering and Events provided the buffet. We were cleaning up when Grant came over to compliment us on the food. Aaron came up and wanted to be introduced to me. Grant was reluctant but did introduce us. Aaron wanted me to stop working and get to know him, but I didn't."

"Has anyone besides Aaron Blalock contacted you?" Sanders asked.

"No," Kelli said. "Why?"

Chief Sanders set a picture of a man on the table, turning it so that both Grant and Kelli could see it.

"Do you recognize this man?" Sanders asked. "Have you seen him at all since the wedding reception?"

Kelli looked at the picture. The man had dark hair and dark eyes. She looked at Grant, who looked back at her. Their eyes locked with curiosity.

"That's the guy who met us on the running trail yesterday morning," Grant said. "He stopped us to ask if we knew what was going on in the park because there were so many people at the entrance."

"I'm sure this is the same guy," Kelli said. She pointed to his right eyebrow. "I spent more time looking at this scar over his eye than I did listening to him."

"Did he do anything besides talk with you?" Sanders asked.

"No," Grant said. "Your communication officer heard the conversation since we had the ear phones in."

"What has this man got to do with Aaron?" Kelli asked.

"His name is Michael VonSinnon," Sanders told them. "This morning, with a lawyer present, Aaron Blalock stated that he worked with this man. Both he and Aaron stalked women, but he said Michael was the leader. Aaron's obsession with Kelli had nothing to do with VonSinnon, but evidently VonSinnon picked up on Aaron's interest and decided to help him out."

"Has he been arrested?" Grant asked.

"No," Sanders said.

"They worked together?" Kelli asked. "How?"

Sanders looked first at Kelli then at Grant.

"We believe VonSinnon used Blalock to obtain the women. Blalock has a record and has been diagnosed as a sociopath with narcissistic tendencies. He was an easy mark for VonSinnon to manipulate.

"He had Blalock do all the kidnapping. VonSinnon had Blalock take the women to a rural cabin on a lake north of Greensboro. I won't go into the sordid details, but you can guess the activities that went on in the cabin. Unfortunately, none of those women have come forward and reported Blalock or VonSinnon. Blalock stated that VonSinnon would send him out to get another woman. He said that when he left, the woman was always still there and alive but was gone when he came back."

Kelli was afraid of the answer, but she had to ask, "Why have those women not said anything?"

"No one has seen those women since they were reported missing," Sanders said. "We have a team of officers and crime scene investigators on the premises of that cabin looking for them or any sign that they were there. We think VonSinnon was responsible for the rape and possible murder of those women. We also believe he didn't involve Blalock in the murder because he didn't trust Blalock to stay quiet."

Kelli was speechless. If she hadn't been prepared with the pepper spray last night, she could have been the next victim.

"Do you know where VonSinnon is?" she asked.

"No," Sanders said. "You have confirmed that he has been in Whitlow. We think he was here until Blalock's arrest. You're sure you haven't seen him since yesterday morning in the park?"

"No, we haven't seen him, but we weren't looking for him, either," Kelli said. She thought a moment, "May I have a copy of that picture?"

Sanders handed her the photo. "This is a copy. The original is in my office."

Kelli took the picture.

"I want to keep it. I need to show it to the staff at the café. It's possible he's been in there." Kelli folded the picture and slid it into her purse. After a few more questions, Kelli and Grant left the building.

Grant parked Kelli's car behind the bakery, and they walked in the back door.

Candy looked up in surprise and said, "I didn't know you two were gone. Did you go to the police department?"

"Yes," Kelli said. She pulled the photo from her purse. "Have you seen this man in the bakery?"

"No," Candy said, "but I mostly work back here. Why?"

"Aaron Blalock told the police that he works with this man," Kelli answered. "The police are looking for him, too."

Candy shook her head with a disgusted grimace.

"Let's go ask Ellen," she said.

Candy, Grant, and Kelli walked to the front of the bakery.

Kelli showed Ellen the picture and asked, "Has this man been in the bakery in the last two or three days?"

"Yes," Ellen said, looking at the picture. "He bought breakfast here yesterday morning and this morning. Why?"

"Did you see which way he went when he left?" Candy asked.

"No. Is there a problem?" Ellen asked.

"Not at all. The police are looking for him. If he comes back in, just sell him what he wants, then call the police when he leaves," Candy instructed her.

"He seemed so nice," Ellen said.

Kelli looked at Candy, "I want to take this over to the café. Tracy or one of the waitresses may have seen him."

"Good idea," Candy said. Candy looked over at Grant, who was wearing an unreadable expression on his face.

"Grant, are you all right?" she asked.

"I thought this was behind us," Grant said. "I had no idea Aaron had a partner. This is all so unbelievable, revolting, psychopathic, and stressful." He looked at Kelli, "Once again, you don't go anywhere without me until this guy is arrested."

"I'm so sorry, Grant," Kelli said, trying to hide a smile. "It seems you just can't get rid of me."

Grant looked at her, grinned, and said, "I guess we all have some sort of cross to bear."

Kelli playfully punched him in the arm.

"Come on," she said. "Walk your burden across the street. The sooner this guy is caught, the sooner we get back to our regular lives. I want to give this picture to Tracy then go to the hardware store for more pepper spray."

"Good idea," Grant said. "Maybe you should carry a candlestick, too. This guy deserves a concussion."

Kelli rolled her eyes at him, then grinned. "Maybe so."

Michael VonSinnon sat at a window table in Candy's Café. He could see the street for a block in either direction. He knew Kelli was working somewhere in the bakery building. He had been in there the last two mornings, but he still had not seen her. Kelli was the most beautiful woman they had targeted yet.

Aaron had been useful to Michael ever since they met at the casino in Cherokee. Aaron was easy to manipulate and convince that he was smooth with the ladies. There had been no denying that some women found Blalock handsome, whereas he was definitely not in the attractive category. That scar across his eye ruined everything.

He had called Aaron to find another woman, but Aaron had resisted. He had become completely obsessed with Kelli Mills. Now that he'd seen Kelli, he was glad. It was too bad Aaron had been arrested. Kelli would be his last woman in this state, then it would be time to move. He didn't trust Aaron to keep his mouth shut about their partnership.

Michael bent over his plate and turned his face toward the window. It was a habit he had developed to keep his face hidden. That scar was too memorable. He never shifted or moved a muscle when he saw Kelli and the man whom he considered her guard dog coming out of the bakery. He smiled. They would be lowering their defenses since Aaron had been arrested. Even if they saw him, they only knew him as an anonymous runner in the park.

Kelli stopped at the bakery door.

"We need to pretend we are relieved and carefree," Kelli said, placing her palm on Grant's chest and leaning into him. "If this Michael VonSinnon is watching, he needs to think we don't know about him."

"I agree. Relieved and carefree, coming up." Grant smiled and held the door for Kelli. She came out, looked up at him with a big smile and took a deep breath. Grant smiled back and gave her a sideways hug. Kelli casually took his hand as they walked across the street leisurely, as if they didn't have a care in the world.

Michael smiled to himself. They obviously didn't know about him, or they would have been nervous and looking around. He watched the door open, and the couple entered then walked to the back of the café.

Kelli went straight to Tracy's office.

Tracy looked up, surprised. "Hey. I thought you would be working across the street, and it's a little early for lunch. Didn't they arrest Aaron Blalock?"

Grant closed the office door. Kelli took out the picture

and laid it on Tracy's desk.

"Don't act any different than you would if I had brought you a catering schedule," Kelli said. "It turns out that Aaron had a partner."

Kelli pointed to the picture, "This man. His name is Michael VonSinnon, and he has already been in the bakery twice in the last two days."

Tracy looked at the picture and did not look up.

"He's in the back dining room right now," she said. "I took his order to help Sylvia."

Grant left the office and walked out of the cafe into the back entryway. Sitting on the steps to his apartment, he called the police department and let them know that Michael VonSinnon was eating in the café.

Two plainclothes detectives were currently eating lunch at Candy's. They were told in their ear radios that the suspect was in the extra dining room. They saw him but kept eating as if nothing had changed.

When a booth directly across the extra dining room opened, Kelli and Grant sat in it and ordered lunch. Michael watched them easily. Kelli and Grant talked with their heads together like they were planning something quietly. Kelli laughed and flipped her hair behind her ears.

Michael grinned. So, the woman liked to flirt. This could be fun.

Michael watched as the couple ate their lunch. When they got up to pay the bill, Michael got up too. He left a large tip, walked to the cash register and got in line behind Kelli and Grant.

Kelli knew Michael was behind them. She also knew there were plainclothes officers in the café and outside on the street. When Grant had paid their bill, they turned.

Kelli looked up at Michael and said, "Oh, hey. I remember you. We saw you in the park the other day." Kelli smiled and flipped her hair as she spoke.

"That's right," Michael smiled. "I'm Michael."

"I'm Kelli," she answered and pointed to Grant. "This is Grant. Maybe we'll meet you on the path again sometime." She looked at Grant, "I guess we need to get back to work."

Looking at Michael she said, "It was nice to meet you." She and Grant walked out the door and started across the street, never looking behind them.

Michael smiled as he came out of the café. The woman would be easy. She thought she already knew him. When Michael stepped out of the door, two men approached him. He politely stepped to the side thinking they were going to enter the cafe. However, to his surprise, he heard them speak.

"Michael VonSinnon, you are under arrest," the officer said.

Just as soon as the words were out of the man's mouth, Michael felt hands grab his arms, pull his hands behind his back and put handcuffs on his wrists.

Across the street Michael saw Kelli and Grant turn around and look at him. The woman had been even cooler than he had. He nodded in acknowledgement. Kelli narrowed her eyes at him, turned, and walked into the bakery.

CHAPTER 27

Inside the bakery, Kelli walked to a table and sat in the chair. She was trembling.

"Are you all right?" Grant asked.

"Yes," she answered. "I'm just so relieved."

Candy came out of the back.

"What happened?" she asked.

Kelli pointed outside the the scene in front of the cafe. Candy watched as Michael VonSinnon was being arrested.

"Does this mean it's over?" Candy asked.

"Finally, it's over," Kelli answered. "It's only been a few weeks, but it feels like it has been months since this began." Kelli smiled, "Looks like I'm working Saturday evening after all."

Candy said, "I guess you are, and I had better get back to the cake I'm decorating for that reception."

Later that afternoon, Hank Bowen entered the bakery's building and went to the third floor. He found Grant and Kelli and asked for a conference in Grant's office. He let them know he had news.

"Michael VonSinnon has been charged with kidnapping, rape, and murder," Hank told them. "The remains of several of his victims were found buried on the grounds of that cabin north of Greensboro."

Kelli felt her stomach drop and the room started to spin. She closed her eyes and put a trembling hand to her mouth.

Grant saw the color drain from Kelli's face and her hands begin to tremble. Afraid she was going to pass out, he eased her onto the couch in his office.

"Are you all right, Kelli?" Hank asked with concern as he watched Grant help her sit down.

Kelli nodded. "Those poor women. They must have been terrified."

She looked at Hank, "Thank you so much. If it weren't for you and your department, that could have been me." Kelli felt tears falling down her cheeks.

Grant was sitting on the couch next to Kelli and put his arm around her.

"You're safe, Kelli," he said. "Remember that."

"I know," she answered, "but hearing that takes the danger I was in to a whole new level. I thought it was just a case of stalking. I completely underestimated the lengths Aaron would go to get his way, and then we find out about Michael VonSinnon."

"They can't get out of jail, can they?" Kelli asked Hank, a look of fear returning to her face. "They can't get out and target me, can they?"

"No," Hank said, trying to reassure Kelli. "They were both denied bail and have already been transferred to the prison in Raleigh where they will wait for trial in North Carolina. Law enforcement agencies in other states are looking at VonSinnon as a suspect in missing person cases, too. So, if he's charged there, he may be transferred for other trials which will increase his incarceration time."

Kelli relaxed and took a deep breath, "Good."

Hank looked at Kelli and Grant, "Thank you for all of your help. Without you two, both Blalock and VonSinnon would still be free. You can expect to be called as witnesses for their trials, but that won't be for a while yet. Life can get back to normal."

Officer Bowen shook hands with both Kelli and Grant and left.

Kelli looked at Grant with a weak smile.

"Well. I guess that's it." She stood, took a deep breath and said, "I have an appointment in a few minutes."

Grant watched her walk back to her office, marveling at the inner strength Kelli had and realizing how lucky he was to have her in his life.

When Kelli and Grant got off work, they ordered take-out plates from the café and went upstairs to eat. Kelli was cleaning the island where they had eaten, and Grant came up behind her.

Grant pulled her into his arms and just held her quietly, hoping to convey that she was safe and that he cared for her.

"I'm glad this ordeal with Aaron and his partner is over," he said. "Are you beginning to feel safe again?"

Kelli wrapped her arms around Grant in a hug. Then she broke the embrace.

"Yes," she said. "It may take a little while, but I feel safe enough that I can pack up and go back to my place. Normal, on the other hand, may take longer."

"I don't think normal will ever be the same," Grant said. "We can't experience what we did and just go back like nothing happened. Normal, everyday working may be the same, but there is one thing I don't want to change."

"What?" Kelli asked.

"Your being here. Will you stay?" Grant asked. He took her hands and looked her in the eyes. "Throughout this whole ordeal, I have had growing feelings for you. I get excited when I wake up and know that you're one of the first people I will see. I love sharing meals with you, talking about our day. I want to make plans with you for the future. Will you stay?"

"Yes," Kelli said. She smiled and squeezed Grant's hands. "I feel the same, Grant. I know I rolled my eyes at you about having to stay here at the start of all this, but I was secretly excited about it. I love being with you, talking with you, working with you. Everything."

Grant sighed, "Good. I don't know what I would have done if you had said no. I just don't want you out of my life, Kelli."

Grant locked eyes with Kelli and dropped to one knee.

"I have fallen in love with you, Kelli Mills. Will you marry me and stay in my life forever?"

"Yes, Grant," she said. "I love you, too." Kelli dropped to her knees. She took his face in her hands and kissed him.

Grant and Kelli took a long weekend, flew to Las Vegas, and came back married. They continued to rent Paul's apartment, stating they liked the commute to their office.

Eventually Garner Logistics moved to the next building and Kelli had the whole third floor above the bakery for Cotton Catering and Events. Kelli smiled as she wrote on her wall calendars, which were now in Grant's old office. That task would never bother Grant again.

In his office on the other side of the third floor, Grant had a shelf where he displayed the can of pepper spray Kelli had used on Aaron and the articles from the newspapers and online news sites. On another shelf, he displayed the candlestick, wall tacks for those calendars, and the topper that had been on their wedding cake. When the time came for him and Kelli to have children, he wanted them to know how brave their mother was, how much he loved her, and how a great love story can come out of difficult beginnings.

ALSO BY A. K. GENTRY

An Awkward Inheritance (Whitlow Series)

An Unlikely Partnership (Whitlow Series)

The Perfect Loophole

About the Author

Having been raised in rural North Carolina, Gentry has lived in small towns and rural settings her whole life. She loves bringing the home town values of family and faith to her books in the Whitlow Series. Gentry is a retired registered nurse. She is married and has two daughters, one son-in-law, two granddaughters and two granddogs.